The Classroom Hopper

Claire Riley

Copyright © 2013 Claire Riley

All rights reserved.

ISBN-13: 978-1493619146

DEDICATION

To Susan D. Bradley,
My Wonderful Grom (Grandma), a writer herself until she passed away too soon earlier this year (2013). I hope that this would have made you proud.

The characters and schools in this book do not resemble real people or real schools. All the characters are fictional, including the main character, Carly Harley, who is not a representation of the author herself. The stories were inspired by Claire Riley's many years of supply teaching.

Claire Riley © 2013.

CONTENTS

Introduction	1
Tuesday Morning	3
Tuesday Afternoon	21
Wednesday	37
Friday Morning	41
Friday Afternoon	71
It was a Monday	83
Another Monday Morning	87
Another Monday Afternoon	117
A Time Waster Day	141
Thursday Morning	145
Thursday Afternoon	181
Saturday Morning	205
Wednesday Morning	207

ACKNOWLEDGMENTS

I would like to offer my heartfelt thanks to my friend, Dan Prosser for his excellent creativity in the form of the book cover.

INTRODUCTION

Most people assume that being a supply teacher means one of three things;
1. You are not a real teacher
2. You are looking for full time work but are incapable of finding it, or
3. You couldn't hack it.

For your information, I'd put myself into category number three. When I say 'I couldn't hack it' – I don't exactly mean that. It's more a case of; I was fed up of devoting every waking hour to my work with little or no recognition and having to suffer terrible school management. Now that I'm a supply teacher, surprisingly, I actually LIKE life. As long as I'm prepared to take a little less remuneration, purchase a few prizes for use as bribes and 'go with the flow', life has markedly improved. It does have its problems however, in that the work is never guaranteed but I take my chances. Having worked in over a hundred schools, I have quite a few stories to tell...

TUESDAY MORNING

It was a Tuesday. The long weekend I'd had due to not receiving a 'morning call' yesterday had not done me any favours. The endless list in my head of possible things I could get done that day raced through my mind like a hamster on a treadmill. Every other minute I looked at the clock. 7:58am. The fridge could do with a clear out. Applying lipstick. 8:00am. I could visit my grandparents. Finding earrings. 8:02am. I've been meaning to... interrupted by my mobile buzzing its way to the edge of the bedside table. A feeling of dread and disappointment crept up from my stomach and into my mouth. It wasn't that I didn't like working ... it was the uncertainty that made it all the more confusing, yet, to keep my sanity, it had to be this way, no eternal ties to any schools, no responsibilities such as lesson planning and staff meetings.

In fact, just the thought of it conjured a picture in my mind of piles and piles of paperwork falling from above, battering me down and causing my demise. I've considered myself as a coward, physically afraid of the workload and commitment and thankfully, I've accepted it as so. The unfortunate thing for me is ... I'm actually a good teacher ... well a good supply teacher anyway.

So, back to the buzzing. Just as the vibrations were about to cease, with a divert to voicemail, my hand snatched the phone and answered it and I'm sure this was without my brain engaging in the first place.

Am I available? Today? Yes I'm available. Which school is it? It was quite a nice school, this could be a satisfactory day. It's year one? Forget it! You know I don't do key stage one, they're just ... so .... er ... unpredictable. Well, I'd rather not give it a go, it could ruin my *brilliant* reputation. Okay. You'll call me again if you get anything in key stage two? Luckily sidestepped. Although now I was feeling quite guilty for not earning the money that I could have earned.

Anyway ... what had I been meaning to do? This was going to bug me now ... another buzzing interruption ... another agency, yes, I'm with quite a lot.

They've personally asked for me? I had no idea why. Year four, village school and only ten minutes up the road? This was the best case scenario I could have wished for. It was now 8:20am. Supposedly, supply teachers should arrive by 8:15am and I had my lunch to make, my teeth to brush and suitable teaching clothes to change into. I was about to perform the maniac 'posing as a headless chicken' routine.

Fortunately, the traffic was rather kind that day and I trundled through the car park at 8:47am. I was not admitted into the building for another twelve minutes though because apparently, in this school, it's imperative for reception staff to attend morning briefings, you know, briefings designed for teachers. It was raining. I was now very wet. By the time I'd signed in the bell had already gone.

After being shown the toilets and the staffroom I arrived at the classroom I would be working in for the rest of the day, and all the children were already sitting smartly on the carpet. The teaching assistant posed confidently as the teacher at the front and shot me a very disapproving look as she glanced up at me after purposefully studying her watch for a second longer than you'd consider normal. I could tell that she was just disappointed that her 'role play' for the day had been foiled.

'Good morning year four,' I announced (I'd never met this class before) 'My name is...'

'My sister says you're Mrs Marley,' shouted a plump, blonde-haired girl sitting on the front row.

'Well technically it's Har...' I attempted in response before being interrupted by her skinny, grinning friend.

'And she told me that you give out prizes!'

'That's true, I do... and you'll find out how...' I began. A wave of whispers filled the room.

'So, we all get one?' yelled a boy from the back corner. He had a typical trouble maker name too.

'No, I'm afraid you have to earn it, and I'll only be choosing two children. So what's your name?'

'Bailey innit,' he replied. Of course it was! He had to be Bailey, Byron or Bryce. There was just something about boys whose name began with 'B'.

Anyhow, they'd destroyed my 'usual' spiel that goes something a little like this (For effect, read my speeches to the children with a bouncy voice – intonation up and down and up and down);

Good morning year four, my name is Mrs Harley.

Please remember that I have thirty names to learn and I learn thirty every day. Personally, I think I'm getting quite good at it, but perhaps today will not be such a good name learning day so you'll really have to help me out. After I've told you this very important thing, I will do my best to remember all of your names.

Now, I have been to hundreds of schools but I've never been to this school before/only been here a few times before (delete as appropriate) and I've been told that you are the best class in the school! Is this true? (Hopefully they'll reply with yes.) Well I do hope that you'll prove it to me. Imagine how nice it would be if I could say that this was the best class I had ever taught! I'm really hoping for a nice day at 'Blah Blah Blah School' so I can tell all my friends how brilliant it is.

Now, in my bag, I have a special box, and I take this special box around with me to all the schools I go to. Inside it are lots of lovely things. (Get out box and hold it up, moving arm around in a semi-circle. If spiel is working, children strain necks to see inside. If spiel is working exceptionally well, an 'ahh' can also be heard.) I am going to choose two children, only two, at the end of the day to pick a prize from my box. Now children, what kind of things do you think you will be doing to win a prize from my box? Please don't say 'well behaved'. What does good behaviour look like? (At this point, everyone's got a good suggestion from sitting sensibly and working hard to not going up to someone and slapping them in the face or not stamping on someone's foot.)

Providing there's no assembly, I then proceed to waste another fifteen minutes learning all the names, back and forth around the class, saying each name at least ten times. The kids quite like it and I usually get a clap at the end. It always amuses me how the children assume that when you've learnt their name once you'll remember it and that you don't have to purposefully learn the names. If that was the case, everyone would be brilliant at times tables. There's an obvious reason for learning all their names though, other than killing fifteen minutes ... knowing names gives ULTIMATE POWER!

Anyway, back to Tuesday. It was time for assembly and we were already late. I lined the class up and we all trailed into the assembly hall, following the lead of a child I'd picked out as hopefully sensible ... the teaching assistant had, um, disappeared? The children stood there smartly, awaiting my approval to be seated. Of course, it's hard to judge on the first glance at a new hall, so the children were all squashed up when they sat down. It's a usual occurrence on my days in random schools. I quickly moved three boys who were sat on top of each other, trying not to attract too much attention from the other teachers, who were sat there impatiently after having their classes seated for five minutes now, in perfect rows of no more than twelve children.

Sheepishly, I stood to the side because there were no chairs left, they just hadn't got one out for me, until one of the teaching assistants gave up their chair for me and found another one. Finally, the assembly began and of course the head teacher leading the assembly had to tell the whole school how she'd be rushing through her assembly because year four were so late.

The good thing about boring assemblies when you're on supply (don't get me wrong, they're not all boring) is that you can get a good look at the kids in the class. Seek out the rebels and the tell-tales just by watching them. If I've learnt their names beforehand I usually take the opportunity to stare at each child and try to remember their names in my head. I do sometimes worry that one day a question will be directed at me, asking what the assembly was actually about. I can get lucky though! Sometimes the police come to visit or the fire brigade or even the mayor. I have to say, sometimes I think I'm very privileged. I've seen loads of free plays, and once a bird of prey display visited the school hall and one of the birds refused to go back to the handler.

As I was glaring at some of the children at the far side of the room, who were now whispering to one another, willing them to look my way (as if my glare would actually cause them to look at me?) two boys who were sat next to me must have had a small kafuffle. Unfortunately, it happened to be the boys I had moved earlier. One had nudged the other and then the other had hit him back. I obviously hadn't noticed this as I was too busy glaring at the girls chattering across the room. The head teacher giving the less than interesting assembly at the front made an elaborate point about the boys' behaviour, ordering them back at playtime, blah, blah, blah, mentioning how they shouldn't be sat together and they *knew* that (although I didn't, but I was made to feel like I should) and how they should be impressing their 'supply teacher' – yes that's my name, supply teacher - while I just sank down into my uncomfortable plastic chair a little more. Oh, the embarrassment. I could feel the other adults in the room glower over at me disapprovingly... What was she doing? I mean, those boys are right in front of her and there she is, staring at the other side of the room... typical of a 'supply teacher'. It wasn't worth reasoning.

Finally, the assembly was over and I was looking forward to feeling 'in control'. As usual, we were the last class to be instructed to leave the assembly hall as the head teacher dismissed each class one by one using the teacher's name and then rather than find out my name or even use the absent teachers, she said to us, 'and this class'. All thirty-one of us traipsed back to class and I barked at them to sit on the carpet. The next stock speech had to be given ...

'Oh dear, children. I am certainly not feeling that this class is the best in the school. In fact, I think this class could possibly be the worst in the school. I don't usually go into reception classes, but I feel like I must be in one now. I am so very disappointed. This is the first time I've been in this class, imagine how I must feel! And boys, hitting each other in assembly ... it's not acceptable is it? I'm embarrassed now. Your head teacher was very cross. That makes me look like I don't know what I'm doing. I don't think I'm going to have a very good day. I'm not sure if I want to give out a prize at the end of the day now. I suggest you go and get your reading books and we shall read silently for twenty minutes.' Speeches like this are usually followed by a wander to the back of the classroom, facing the wall so I can have a snigger, and this day was no different.

There was a reason the children were reading independently for twenty minutes, and it wasn't really because of the behaviour in assembly, it was so I could work out what we were going to do. I started perusing the planning sheet that had been left out for me. Apparently, the deputy head had taken due care and attention to help me out this morning by going onto the system and printing it out for me. Okay, Literacy.

According to the planning, the children were supposed to be writing part three of a five part story. This really is the worst thing you can get for Literacy on supply and it's *literally* impossible. The teacher will never get the outcome that lies inside his or her own mind unless they themselves deliver it. It's like saying, guess the story I've just made up in my head and write the middle bit down.

To start the lesson off, a sequence of pictures needed to be shown. This sequence of pictures was on an interactive whiteboard program on the computer and the file was saved on the absent teachers memory stick, at her house. Hmmm. So that caused quite a large problem. I contemplated drawing a series of pictures, although I had no idea what they should be and then sensibly (so I thought anyway) made the executive decision to go with something different. Out of my bag I pulled my trusty Literacy skills book. There's always something the kids can't do ... usually it's using capital letters and full stops, no joke! I found a few appropriate pages for all levels and waited patiently for the teaching assistant to return.

By this time the children had been reading for twenty-three minutes and they were beginning to get quite restless. The teaching assistant was still nowhere to be found so I decided that it was time to change activity. When I announced to the children that we were going to be playing *heads down, thumbs up*, excitement rippled around the room and most children sat up smartly with arms folded as tall as they possibly could – I'm sure they believe the taller they are, the more you can see them and the more likely you are to choose them ... nothing to do with their behaviour so far that day. Just after we had begun playing, the teaching assistant finally re-emerged. I talked her through my decision and showed her the pages I wanted photocopying.

'If the teacher wants them to write a story, then that's what they should be doing. They get enough fun, we shouldn't be doing fun things,' she trumpeted.

'Okay,' I replied, (I wasn't aware that children found punctuation fun) 'I can understand that, but in this situation we are rather stuck. It is better if they're actually learning something useful, like punctuation, rather than struggling through a lesson with no resources - and me today - and then re-doing it with resources and their teacher tomorrow. That won't be helpful to anyone, especially the ill teacher.'

'Well I can't leave the classroom in lesson times and we're not allowed to use the photocopier.' Then where the heck had she been all this time?

'What?'

'Yes, only the teachers have photocopy cards because apparently we can't be trusted. The teacher keeps it in the drawer over there.' She pointed to the desk and I was beginning to realise that her problem wasn't necessarily with me.

'Alright,' I responded, wondering whether or not I was actually speaking with an adult, 'well I'm giving you permission to use the teacher's photocopying card to do some photocopying for me. I'm sure they'll understand given the circumstances.'

Eventually, I'd talked her into it and returned my attention to the children, who seemed to be running the game pretty sensibly between themselves. At that moment, the head teacher entered the room.

'I just wanted to see how you were getting on,' she

said, peering up at the clock. 'Haven't you been left any Literacy planning?'

'Ah, well,' I stammered, 'There are no resources so I've just sent Mrs Hodley to the photocopier...' What had I done? Not only had I just dropped myself in it, but the teaching assistant as well.

'I see,' and with that she left the room and closed the door behind her.

With the worksheets finally in my hand, we began the lesson, much to the disappointment of Bailey, as he had only just stood up at the front for his turn to squeeze someone's thumb.

'Right children. Today we are going to be practicing using the correct punctuation, the right punctuation in our sentences,' I started. I repeated myself in a slightly different way deliberately as it was essential for at least half of the class! On the board I wrote the following sentence:

i like playing with my friend jason

'Now, children, can you spot the places where I have not used the correct punctuation, the right punctuation?' (It is always tricky as I'm never really sure what they already know. They could fly through it or look at me as if I'm explaining Pythagoras' Theorem, and their age really doesn't count for anything when you are used to moving around from school to school.) A curly-haired ginger boy shot his hand up and tried to make his body stretch up as high as he could. I was going to choose him to give an answer until I noticed a shorter boy next to him doing the same, but also holding his breath and going rather red. I thought I best choose the second boy to prevent me having to deal with a first aid incident. 'Yes, what do you think?'

He swallowed and caught his breath before responding, 'Capital letter!'

'Yes, okay, but where?'

'I.'

'Excellent, and why is that?'

'Because it's at the beginning.'

'That's right. Can anyone tell me the other reason why 'I' would need a capital letter?'

'Full stop!' shouted Bailey.

'I'll just ignore that, Bailey,' I growled. 'First of all, it's not the answer to the question I asked, and secondly you've shouted out. I think you should have learnt about putting your hand up in reception class.' I collected answers from a few more students and they also gave me answers that were not the answer to the question. When I'd exhausted the children with hands up, I picked on a shy little girl (I'm mean, I know) hoping she wouldn't burst into tears on me, because it happens, usually without warning and you can never tell if they'll be a crier or not.

'Because 'I' always has a capital when it's on its own,' she offered sheepishly.

'Fantastic! Ten house points for you.'

'We don't have house points, Miss.'

'Er, sorry ... I mean, ten merits for you,' I replied apologetically. The girl grinned from ear to ear, I had no idea that receiving ten merits was so good. Later on the teaching assistant informed me merits were only given out in singles once a term for exceptional work. Oops.

Next we tried a harder sentence, which we talked through, and then the children tried it on their own white boards. This was the sentence:

hello said mr bond how are you today

As I walked around the room I clocked some *excellent* responses;

Hello "said Mr Bond" how are you today?

"Hello" said Mr Bond "How" "are" "you" "today"

Mr Bond wondered how you was today

hallo mr bend who ar yoo tudai

Ten minutes of practicing punctuating in books followed while I raced around the room from raised hand to raised hand with my trusty green pen, tick, tick, ticking away as I went. By this time, I was getting pretty fed up, I was really in need of a break but I had no idea what time playtime was. 10:29am ... was it possible? Suddenly, a beautiful sound was heard, the bell.

Ushering them out of the classroom as quickly as possible so that I could actually eat breakfast and mark a few books to knock some minutes off the end of my day, I noticed the children waiting at the door of the cloakroom, not going outside. I padded over to them, after all, we all needed the break after the stressful morning we'd had.

'We can't go out without a teacher,' whined the plump blonde girl. The snot hanging from her nose, threatening to dive on the floor, gave me a strange sense of urgency.

'Yes, I can understand that, sounds like a sensible idea to me,' I assured her. 'Let me see if I can find out what's happening.' I spotted Mrs Hodley skipping towards the staffroom happily with her travel mug and a banana. 'Mrs Hodley,' I called. 'There's no teacher outside so the children can't go out.'

'Well there won't be yet,' she replied gleefully. 'It's your duty.'

Well of course it was! Why wouldn't it be? If I was

there on a Tuesday it would be my duty, if I was there on a Friday it would be my duty, in fact, any day would be my duty because a supply teacher is always on duty! I don't know if you know this, but supply teachers have bladders made of steel and they never need a break, or a drink for that matter, otherwise they'd need to go to the toilet at break times instead of covering Tom, Dick and Harry's duties.

Feeling guilty that I'd held the children up for so long, I dashed back to the classroom to get my coat and opened the door to the outside world. The children spurted out like tons of water flowing through an open door in the Titanic. 10:36am and I was still supervising four classes on my own in heavy drizzle. To my surprise, two more adults then sauntered out, travel cups teeming with hot coffee and a cake for 'Brenda from the office's birthday' in tow.

A tall for her age, dark-haired girl from year one (aged five or six) followed me around the playground asking me how old I was, how many children I had and how long I'd been teaching. Every time I edged away to escape, she noticed and came bounding over again. At one point, I even tried hiding around the corner of the bike shed, but she scoured the playground with a friend until she tracked me down. She was less than impressed with my answers (the ones I give to every question of this type). I'm one hundred and seven, I have fifty children and I've been teaching for seventy-six years. Apparently I only look like I'm eighteen and it couldn't be possible that I'm so old because I'm not sporting any wrinkles. I did explain though, how using a nightly aging cream has made all the difference for me. In case you were wondering, my age at the time of writing this book is actually twenty-eight.

Then came the customary stare from the other adults in the playground. Obviously, I'd had a somewhat useless teaching assistant and I'd arrived after there was time to consult anyone else on important matters, so I had no flipping idea what time break finished, I'd only just found out what time it started!. After the children had gained a few more cheeky minutes of extra play, one of the adults strode over to me purposefully. 10:47am.

'Well, are you going to do the whistle?' she snapped.

'Wouldn't it be better coming from you, as after all, you know the routine of the school?' I replied.

'I don't have a whistle,' she sneered. 'It's the teacher's job and you're the teacher on duty.' Despite the fact that I could see that it would be more effective for a known member of staff to carry out this task with a hundred twenty children I didn't know, I went ahead anyway.

'So how do you blow it?' I asked.

'What?' She looked at me in disgust, perhaps she thought I was implying something rather rude. (I do know how to blow a whistle by the way.)

'What routine do you have? Blow once? Twice? Do you do it with an inflection? Do you do it 'Captain of a ship style'? Do they have to stop and stand still first? Do they line up? Do they just walk straight in? I am expecting them to be in a line of boys and girls? Will they be in houses? Will the teachers come out or do we just trail them all in?' Now, I could see how my question had been a sensible one, but I could understand her confusion with this school being the centre of the universe.

'Blow once and they'll line up,' she huffed. 'The teachers will come out.'

11:11am and we were finally sat on the carpet. Not me, the children. If you're any good at Maths, then perhaps you'll have realised that twenty-four minutes to get from the playground to the carpet is a rather long time. It *was* a long time. Mrs Longbottom, the year six teacher did her photocopying for the next lesson after break time while I stood outside gormlessly in the cold with two rowdy classes, waiting for someone to turn up and let us in. We'd been waiting so long that we'd been locked out. I must point out though, that this was perfectly acceptable on Mrs Longbottom's part (according to her) because as a year six teacher, she had *the* most important job in the school (and for the school that's at the centre of the universe – it's saying a lot).

I was bursting for the toilet. During the first session I'd swigged coffee desperately from my faithful travel cup at regular intervals to keep the caffeine levels high. I'm sure you'll be really surprised to find out that I was waiting for Mrs Hodley to grace us with her presence. 11:22am and I'd exhausted my extensive list of time waster questions and knew the name of every child's cat, dog, brother, mother, sister, dad, cousin, auntie, uncle and lizard. She waltzed in at 11:23am.

'Mrs Hodley,' I cooed, 'I was hoping you could do me a massive favour. As I've been on duty, I thought that you could get them organised in their Maths tables with their Maths groups. I've written the learning objective on the board for the children to copy into their books. I really need the toilet.'

'The children aren't allowed to go in lesson,' she remarked cockily. 'I really don't think it would set a good example for the children.' What was it with this woman?! Why did she hate me so much?

'I can see your point, Mrs Hodley, but in all fairness, they've actually had the time to go at break time, as have you,' I said through gritted teeth, trying not to let too much spit escape from my mouth and spray all over her, although it would have been satisfying. Under duress, she gave in.

I hopped frantically to the toilet as by this time I was more than desperate, praying I would not bump into the head teacher on the way.

Reaching for the ladies toilets door, I was suddenly startled as it was yanked open from the other side, moments before I made contact. The head teacher emerged and barged past me forcefully. Immediately, I looked at my practical school shoes, like a defenceless child who'd been sent to her office, willing the ground to swallow me whole.

At 11:27am I was back in the classroom, I really hadn't been long, I daren't be!

Due to the fact I was having such a terrible day, and the fact I couldn't count on any adult help, I decided to make the next lesson a marking free lesson – in other words, they write it on their whiteboards and then we rub it out! Besides, with all the faffing around (which you can plainly see, was not my fault) we only had half an hour until lunch time.

'Right Children, (don't forget the bouncy voice) in Numeracy today we're going to be looking at number facts we already know and how we can use them to help us do more difficult sums. First of all I'd like you write out the following sums with their answers.' On the board I wrote;

2 + 3 =
7 + 9 =
13 + 4 =
6 + 12 =

'This is well easy, Miss!' roared Bailey. If only it was! Little Jimmy on blue table had written 2 + 3 = 6.

'Mrs Hodley, could you come and give some support on blue table please?' I was focused now, I was going to make her work! 'Hold up your whiteboards please.' The majority of the class had added correctly. I breathed a sigh of relief. 'So if we know that 2 + 3 = 5 then what else do we know? What about 20 + 30?' Fortunately for me, they'd done some work on this two weeks previously, so the bright ones picked it up fairly quickly. After a few more questions I wrote fifty questions on the board. When they'd done ten they had to get an adult to check and then rub them out and do the next ten. Boy, I was going to have some fun!

Small, holding breath, red-faced boy was first to put his hand up. At the time I was still thinking up questions.

'Mrs Hodley,' I called knowingly. 'A little help over here please.' I pointed at the boy and she gave me a dirty look before toddling over. Next, Bailey had his hand up. 'Mrs Hodley, Bailey needs your help.' Then, as I predicted, all of blue table had their hands up. 'Mrs Hodley, the whole of your table is rather confused, go and help them,' I commanded. At this point, the curly-haired ginger boy approached me with his whiteboard. 'Are you wanting to have your work checked?' He nodded. 'Mrs Hodley, Ben's work needs checking.' She stood up angrily, causing the chair to almost fall over, and scowled as she stamped over to Ben's table. I felt a small amount of revengeful satisfaction. 'Right children, please finish off the last question you are doing, lunchtime is in one minute.'

The children tidied up their tables pretty quickly and sat smartly whilst staring me down, trying to telepathically instruct me to release them first. The bell rang and Mrs Hodley collected her coat from the work surface just next to the door, where she'd put it a minute earlier to 'get ready', and exited the room. We waited for the dinner lady to collect them, at least that's what I'd been lead to believe would happen anyway.

Five minutes later, at 12:05, the dinner lady strolled in casually and took the class to wash their hands. Peace at last!

TUESDAY AFTERNOON

I took the opportunity to pay another visit to the ladies room so that I would be able to mark the books and eat my lunch with no interruptions when I got back. This makes me sound really unsociable, I know, but I've realised that making friends in the staffroom means leaving school really late and then I haven't gained anything by being in such an unstable role. It would be the same long hours that I'd done before.

At 12:10pm I floated back into the classroom happily, hang on a minute, what was this? Kids in my room! Was it wet play? No it was not! They were munching away at their sandwiches.

'What's going on here then?' I scowled. 'Why are you in the classroom at lunch time?'

'We always eat in the classroom, Miss, everyone on sandwiches does because there's not enough room in the hall,' said Anetta, a lovely girl who had caused me no problems all day. I could feel my blood starting to simmer, but I did try to keep a lid on it, for her sake.

'Okay, so where is the dinner lady that's supposed

to be supervising you?'

'She just comes in sometimes and sometimes the teacher's here.' ARRRGGGGHHHHHHH!!!!!! I was at screaming point, but I held it in. I contemplated going to the staffroom and facing the mindless conversation about this kid and that kid who I had no idea about or the latest revolutionary idea to pop up in the weekly staff meeting. No. It was better to just soldier on as if this chaos was not spilling out of control around me.

I ambled over to my bag and pulled out my lunchbox, then sat down with it at one of the children's desks with the pile of Literacy books I'd had the children leave open for me on the correct page, to make it quicker. Out of my pencil case I extracted one of my twenty-six green pens. Cleverly, I'd done most of the ticking in class, so it was just a case of writing a comment on each piece of work. I've realised over the years that it's a good idea to work out what your three comments will be, (never admit that though) then you can always adjust them as appropriate. Usually they are only half truths as you have to make them all sound *positive* somehow.

I'd commented on two of the books and chucked them on the floor as a note to myself that I'd marked them when Little Jimmy, who was still munching his way through his strawberry jam sandwiches, decided that I would be his friend this lunch time. This is exactly what I was trying to avoid... with adults, never mind children.

'Miss, are you married?' he asked in his small, squeaky voice.

'Usually, Jimmy, when a person is called Mrs, that means they're married. So, what do you think? Am I married?'

'Er... do you have a husband?'

'Well if I was married, I'd have a husband, and to be married I have to be called Mrs and my name is Mrs Harley isn't it? So yes, Jimmy, to make it simple, I am married and I do have a husband'. Listen Jimmy, it's nice to have a chat and everything, but the thing is, it's my break time now and I really need to get lots of work done and I have to do that without talking, so if you could just chat quietly to the people on your table, that would be great.' He looked at me with puppy dog eyes as if I'd ripped his heart out and stomped all over it. I really just didn't have the time to be babysitting.

I continued with the books, only twenty-eight more to go. Sometimes, I'm that sad that I arrange them in piles of five so I can quickly count up how many are left after every couple I've done. 12:25pm, must fit lunch in. After taking the first bite of my ham sandwich, I looked up to see the children staring at me, sandwiches in their hands, mouths open (some of them didn't swallow first either). Yes, the alien teacher was eating, and guess what, she was eating the same as us, sandwiches!

By 12:30pm, half of the children had gone out to play, leaving only the slow eaters, of which I was one. I'd only eaten that one bite out of my sandwich. I was starving and willing them to hurry up so I could eat without being watched.

Big Henry was sat opposite little Jimmy and he kicked him under the table out of boredom. Little Jimmy attempted to kick him back but his little legs couldn't reach. I caught a glimpse and giggled under my breath, watching his legs flailing about under the table. I wasn't getting involved, that was why the dinner lady should have been in the room. It was my lunch time for goodness sake, they'd already robbed me of a break!

Little Jimmy slid under the table, crawled over to big Henry and punched him in the leg and big Henry retaliated by kicking little Jimmy in the face. That was it, it had started.

'Right you two!' I bawled. 'Jimmy, take your lunch and eat it at the table in the corner, Henry, you come and eat your lunch next to me.' At that moment, the dinner lady finally popped her head around the door.

'Ah, I can see you've got it all under control here, Miss,' she remarked as she wandered off into the distance. Typical! It wasn't even my responsibility to be sorting them out and now I'd be lumbered with them all lunch time. If I didn't stick to my guns and make an example of them, the afternoon would be so much harder.

Twenty-five books left to mark, 12:40pm. I'd only cleared another two before it started again.

'Miss, what's your cat called?'

'I'm busy, Jimmy.'

'I know, but I was just trying to remember what he was called.'

'Stig. I really need to mark these books, Jimmy.'

'Stig's a funny name.' I replied with silence. 'I like the name Stig.' More silence. 'My cat's called Bubbles.'

'Okay boys, I think you've stayed in long enough. There are fifteen minutes of playtime left, I don't want to hear that you've been silly again.' I couldn't hack it anymore. They left immediately and I was childless once again.

It was a rushed job, but with no interruptions and my brain and hand working double speed I managed to mark another ten books and eat the rest of my sandwiches, a yoghurt and a chocolate biscuit before 12:58pm.

I was also on time to collect the children from the playground. We followed year five very closely so as not to get locked out, leaving year six in the playground once again, this time with the dinner ladies. Mrs Longbottom was probably doing some more photocopying, after all, she couldn't possibly trust her teaching assistant to do it. Things were looking up. The afternoon was going to be much more successful!

Taking the register ran smoothly and Mrs Hodley took interventions all afternoon so we didn't have her in the class (probably why she was the way she was – almost a teacher). Everything was going to plan. We were also in for what would hopefully be an easy lesson in the ICT suite ... typing up the first two parts of the story they had written previously.

Once everyone had a pencil, their Literacy book, and were lined up in alphabetical order we set off to the computer room at the other end of the school. Every twenty steps or so we had to stop and wait for the stragglers to catch up, Bailey's last name was Watson, so he was one of them.

On arrival at the ICT room, I was just about to take a look at the room before giving out instructions when I was approached by a stern looking woman. I thought she was going to tell me that we couldn't use the ICT suite, but instead, she stood there in the doorway and beckoned the children one by one. As they approached her, they showed her their hands just like the seven dwarves.

'Two,' she barked, 'seven, nine.' It turned out that she was instructing them which computer to go to.

Oooh, I liked this ... I could feel a relaxing session coming up, hopefully she'd be teaching the lesson. I could send someone for those books that I hadn't yet marked. 'Bailey, wash those hands with *soap* in the toilets then join the back of the line.' He was already supposed to be at the back wasn't he? I could count on Bailey to push in.

'So, are you the ICT teacher then?' I asked.

'I am.'

'What would you like me to do in the lesson then?'

'Ha! I don't teach this class! The ICT co-ordinator insists on teaching her own!' (So the teacher I was covering must have been the co-ordinator.)

'Ah, so you'll be leaving us then?'

'Oh no, I'll just stay and get on with my paperwork. Just pretend I'm not watching.' Oh great! So I had to teach an ICT lesson on a system I didn't know in front of a specialist who did know and she blatantly just told me she'd be watching... What was that I said about things looking up?

'Okay children, could we have all arms folded and looking this way please,' I requested calmly.

Big Harry chipped in, 'Mrs Heightler says we have to have our hands in the air.' I would have loved to ignore that but I could feel her eyes on me. I glanced over and she raised her eyebrows as if to say, 'well, do it then'.

'Alright, hands in the air please children. Today in your ICT lesson you are going to be typing up the stories you have been writing in Literacy. This will help you to get faster at typing and give you a better knowledge of where the letters are on the keyboard. The first thing I'd like you to do is log on...'

'You need to show them what to do first, then they log on,' Mrs Heightler interrupted. 'You can use this computer next to me and it'll show up on the screen.'

There was something about the name Heightler that reminded me of an infamous and dangerous dead leader. She was displaying some of his qualities too.

I stepped over to the computer next to her. 'Okay ... so ... the first thing you need to do after you've logged on in to open Word...'

'We use Works in this school.'

'I mean Works, and you can find it in, hang on a minute...' It wasn't on the start menu. I opened the search box and began searching for it.

'It's on the desktop, plain as day, Works!'

'Oh, of course, if you just look at the screen, you can see Works here.' I circled the icon with my cursor. I'm generally very good with ICT, but this woman was making me look like an idiot with her comments and the way she was watching me was making me all jittery and turning me to jelly. 'Now, once you have it open you can begin typing. We are not messing around changing any fonts until you've typed everything up. Please remember to use capital letters and full stops. How do we make a letter a capital using the keyboard?'

Little Jimmy had his hand up. I nodded at him to respond. 'Caps lock.'

'Well done, Jimmy.'

'That's not the only way though is it children?' Heightler butted in once again. 'What is the grown-up way we use to create capital letters Sarah?' Sarah was another child who belonged to the blue table. I was sure she'd chosen her to prove to me that *everyone* knew this one.

'The shit button?'

'Pardon?!' Heightler replied, shocked.

I was finding it really hard to keep the giggles in.

'Did you say shift button?'

Sarah gave a blank stare whilst we both willed her to reply with 'yes'. 'Er... yeah,' she said.

'Excellent,' stuttered Heightler. 'So children, to make a capital letter, I expect you to be using the *shift* button.' Her emphasis was totally on the 'f'. I stared at her to see if she had anything else to say but she turned away and continued looking busy.

'Miss,' I heard from behind me, I predicted the voice. 'My arms are aching.'

'Put them down then, Bailey. Right children, is there anyone who doesn't understand what they're doing?' Bailey still had his hand raised. 'Great, so everyone knows what they're doing, off you go.'

The children had been writing their own stories set in imaginary worlds, but blue group could only cope with retelling a familiar story. Sarah had chosen to retell Cinderella. As I was walking around the classroom on cyber game prevention duty, I was pleased to see that she'd been working hard the whole time and had typed up much of her story. It read as follows: (If you are not a teacher, read it as it sounds to decode.)

Wons upon a tim thair woz a poor girl corld sinderela she woz a cleaner at her mums hows and a pric caym from the casl to giv her a slipr and then the pric went hom the and the pric wonted sinderela to go to the casl and be the prics wif and then she woz a pricess and thay wer pric and pricess togethr

'Sarah,' I asked in alarm, although to be fair, she'd already shown her lack of knowledge of inappropriate language. 'This word here,' I pointed at 'pric,' 'What is it supposed to say?'

'Prince, Miss.'

'Ah, ok. Let's listen to the sounds in prince. See if there's a sound you've missed out. P-r-i-n-ce. Can you spot what you've missed?'

'rrrr?'

'Hmm… listen again, carefully. P-r-i-n-ce.'

'Oh, n?'

'Good girl, that's right. I think it would be a good idea if you look at all the times you've written prince and princess and make sure the 'n' sound is there.' I brought my hands up to my face and gave my forehead a rub, it was turning out to be a long day.

The next screen I noticed was Bailey's. He'd written up the first sentence of his story.

'Bailey, why have you only written one sentence of your story?'

'I've been working on the design, Miss.'

'Yes, I can see that. You've done exactly what I asked you not to do.' Every letter in his sentence was a different colour, each word was in a different font and as you read along the line, the words became bigger. 'I don't think that it's going to be very easy for your reader to read.'

'Well it's my teacher reading it and she's really good at reading weird stuff. She's always saying that my writing is difficult to read.'

'Hmmm… perhaps she's hoping you'll start making it easier for her to read?'

'I don't think so, I heard her telling Mrs Hodley that she wanted a job here because she likes a challenge.' How could I argue with that?

I looked at the clock, 1:40. 'Please finish off the sentence you are writing and save your work.' At that moment, Big Harry leaned back in his seat and then with all his power and might sneezed the biggest sneeze I had ever seen. There was snot all over his monitor, gradually dribbling its way down towards the keyboard. Drip, drip, drip. He stared at the story he'd written, though the view was smeared, and did nothing.

Mrs Heightler jumped out of her seat speedily, reached for her rubber gloves and grabbed the biggest bottle of disinfectant you have ever seen. She shooed Harry to the toilets and set to work, de-germing every nook and cranny. By the time all the children had lined up she'd sprayed it, wiped it and dried it and then proceeded to move up the line of children, and spray hand sanitizer on every child's hands. I was at the end of the line and I got germ-busted too.

As we set off back to class, Harry was coming out of the toilets, wiping his wet hands down the sides of his trousers. Mrs Heightler was waiting for him with a scowl. She summoned him to be sanitised before he could join us back in class.

Back in the classroom, it was time for PSHCE; there's nothing like a good circle time with year four. We all sat around, just like we were sitting around a campfire. I began with a statement before we passed it around.

'I feel happiest when... I am at home playing with my cat. Each person must take it in turns around the circle to finish the sentence, 'I feel happiest when'.'

Sarah was on my left, 'I feel happiest when I am playing with my dog.' Original.

'I feel happiest when I am playing with my friends.'

'I feel happiest when I'm on my Xbox 360.'

'I feel happiest when I'm on my Xbox 360 *and* my

PSP.'

'I feel happiest when I'm on my Xbox 360 *and* my PSP *and* my Wii.'

'You don't even have an Xbox 360,' boy one announced.

'Yeah I do,'

'No you don't, Bailey's been to your house and he says you don't even have a TV in your room.'

'Okay boys,' I interjected. 'I'm sure there are other things that make you happy.' They gave me rather puzzled frowns.

'I feel happy when my Dad goes to work.' Oh dear, not so good.

'Is that because he's earning money to look after you?'

'No, but my mum's always in a much better mood when he's out. I think it's because her secret friend is allowed to stay for a sleepover when he's gone.' I was sorry I asked … something to mention to Mrs Hodley later.

'I feel happy when I have a fight with my sister. I hate her.'

'Hmmm … I don't really think that's something to be happy about, Francesa,' I remarked. This could have spiraled downwards very quickly.

'I feel happiest when I am having a food fight!'

'I feel happy when I'm having a food fight with my brother.'

'I feel happiest when I'm having a food fight at school.'

'Okay children, I think we'll move on to the next activity. On your whiteboards with a partner, I'd like you to think of ten things that would make your parent or carer happy.'

I wandered around the room after they'd started. Bailey hadn't written any words, he'd just drawn a questionable picture. It consisted of two things that were round and one that was long, sitting in the middle. Was it a coincidence that he should have been thinking of things that would make his mum happy?

'And what is that, Bailey?' I demanded. He looked up at me sheepishly over his shoulder as I'd technically crept up on him. 'I'm utterly disappointed in you! What a terrible thing to draw. Rub it off immediately and go and sit on the 'thinking table'.' The thinking table was basically a single desk at the front of the room, so if sat on it properly, you couldn't really see anything or anyone else. He skulked off with his bottom lip trailing on the floor.

There were some lovely responses on some of the children's whiteboards, such as 'tidying my room' and 'emptying the bin'. Little Jimmy had written on his board, 'letting my mum play on my DS' and Sarah thought that her grandma would be happy if she let her sleep on her bedroom floor and have a sleepover. Harry had written three ideas; he would take his mum to the park, watch *Spongebob Squarepants* with her and let her have chocolate and sweets for tea. I'm sure his mum couldn't wait.

2:50pm and it was time to start getting the children ready for home. A swarm of activity ensued with letters and book bags being handed out.

'Make sure you put the letters in your book bags children, I don't want to see any left behind on the tables or under them.' I moved around the class stealthily and checked every child had carried out the instruction.

The children lined up and then we made our way to the cloakroom. They collected their things while I opened the door to the playground and stood guard. Not knowing the children's parents really does slow everything down as you have to stop every one of them and ask them to point out who they are going home with, not that I suppose this would prevent anything terrible from happening if it was going to, but anyway.

Bailey was ready first and it seemed he couldn't wait to get out of school.

'Stop!' I commanded as he tried to push past me. 'Show me who you are going with.'

He pointed to a woman with a face that looked like she was chewing a wasp, standing in the far corner of the playground. She certainly looked like Bailey's mum.

'Okay, off you go.'

Most of the children were collected with no problems, I just had Sarah, Harry and Jimmy left. Sarah had been out three times already. Her mum kept sending her back in for things like her gloves, hat and book bag. Every time she came in to get something she'd forgotten, she left something else behind. I really felt for her mother, standing out in the freezing cold, but I wasn't allowed to let her in, health and safety of staff and students apparently, and I couldn't un-man the door either.

Finally, she managed to collect everything and Harry followed swiftly behind. There was only little Jimmy left and his mother was waiting very impatiently at least half in the doorway. If she stepped any further, I thought I might have to use my arm as a barricade. I've never been a bouncer before, so I was rather apprehensive.

'What's the matter, Jimmy? Are you looking for

something?' I asked gently, although the only thing on my mind was that it was now 3:15pm and I still had Literacy books to mark.

'I've lost my hat,' he whimpered and then looked sheepishly at his mother. Perhaps she was really cross. She was hopping around a bit with her arms folded, but that was probably because she was stupid enough not to wear a coat or a jumper and it was rather cold.

'Why don't we go and have a look in lost property in the hall then?' I moved to the door and waited for his mother to step back and then closed it. Unfortunately it was really heavy and so it slammed, and because she didn't move very far back, it slammed in her face ... oops.

Looking through the lost property, the hat was the first thing we came across.

'That's mine,' he said, taking the hat and putting it on his head. I was just about to walk away when he picked up a scarf. 'That's mine too. Oh and this,' fishing out a red glove.

'Did you lose just the one glove or should we look for the other?'

'We should probably look for the other. My mum says I'm always losing things and she gets cross because the dole don't give her lots of money.'

'I see, well let's have a better look then.' I tipped out the box onto the floor and little Jimmy began sorting all the items. He put one quarter back in the box and kept three quarters of the items. I was worried that this stuff wasn't actually his, but at least his mum could check. There was so much that I put it all in the lost property box, leaving the items he hadn't claimed on the hall floor and took them to his mother who was still freezing outside.

'Jimmy says these are all his... are they?'

She did a thorough check. 'Yep, all his... he's always losing stuff, leaving me skint. He's lost some red underpants too, any chance you've found them?' I looked at Jimmy. How was it possible to lose underpants?! I cocked my head in the direction of the hall, motioning him to go and check. A few seconds later he trailed back with two pairs of underpants, a red pair and a blue pair. 'So you lost the blue pair too?' she scowled.

I held out the box for Jimmy to deposit the underpants in and handed the box to his mum. 'You best take the box with you, looks like you're going to need it for the journey home, just bring it back tomorrow.'

3:30pm and school had finished half an hour previously. I raced back to the classroom, passing a trail of letters all over the corridor. How was that even possible? I personally saw to it that they had been deposited in book bags. I rushed through the remaining Literacy books, tidied the classroom, left a note for the teacher and filled out my timesheet.

By 3:50pm I was at the school office, I handed over my timesheet to be signed and faxed, feeling a little embarrassed as I was probably in some kind of trouble with the head from previous events. Besides, on a supply teacher's first couple of days in a school, the head teacher usually consults the teaching assistant, to see if they're worth having back again. I could kiss goodbye to this school for sure.

Just as I was leaving, the head teacher popped her head around the corner, exactly what I'd been dreading.

'Mrs. Hodley's been singing your praises. Apparently the class' behaviour was ten times better than with their usual teacher, hopefully we'll see you again very soon.' I left the school in a whirlwind of confusion.

WEDNESDAY

Advanced bookings are the best type of supply bookings. Having knowledge of the school and year I'll be going to in advance is really useful and it gives me time to get in a 'work' frame of mind.

On this particular day I was going to a nearby tough school that I had a really good relationship with, I knew lots of the staff and I'd been there hundreds of times. It was an afternoon booking, which was a bit of a pain as you can't usually get a separate booking for the morning, so it's only half a day's pay and you don't really get time for yourself. Anyhow, it was better than nothing and I'd had a good relationship with this school for a while.

I wolfed down my lunch at 11:45, despite the fact I'd only had breakfast two hours previously. Annoyingly, the agency's rule about being there at least thirty minutes before the session starts still applies. This thirty minutes, however, is great for catching up with your exercises as you walk aimlessly around the classroom with nothing to do, re-reading every display and noticing every crack in the paintwork.

I always thought that daytime traffic, especially Monday-Thursday would be pretty quiet until I went on supply and had some weekdays off. I was wrong. I've come to the conclusion that it's a culmination of more pensioners keeping their driving licences and mothers visiting soft play centres in the family's second car. I arrived at school twenty-five minutes before the session started and panic jumped inside me a little. It was always worse when the school phoned the agency to find out where you were and then the agency phoned you, and by the time this had all happened you were ten minutes later than you would have been.

Anyway, no such thing happened that day. I raced through the car-park and strode up to the reception desk.

'Hi Carly, did you forget something last time you were here?' the lady on reception asked.

'Erm, not that I'm aware of...' I answered, feeling a little confused.

'Oh, so why are you here then?'

'I'm in year five today, Mrs Trundle's on a course,' I affirmed confidently. 'The agency told me about it last week, it's been booked for ages.'

'Jane! Jane!' she shouted over her right shoulder. Jane came rushing out.

'Ah yes, it's year five today, Mrs Trundle's class,' Jane said nervously, whilst fumbling around under the counter, looking for my badge (I had a permanent one here because I was such a regular visitor). I was also pleased to be 'right' as the receptionist could be rather difficult at the best of times.

At that moment, Mrs Trundle came galloping down the corridor joyfully as she was making her exit.

'Ah Mrs Trundle, what would you like me to do with your class this afternoon?' I questioned.

'Are you supposed to be taking my class?' she replied in confusion.

'Yes, apparently so, is that a problem?'

'Well, you won't be needed. I've got a student teacher and he's taking the class this afternoon. He knows what he's doing and he's great with the kids.' I'm sure he was … they weren't technically supposed to do that, but never mind.

One minute later and the deputy head had been summoned. 'I'm sorry, Carly, but there's nowhere we can use you this afternoon,' and with that I was dismissed to the car park. I'd wasted at least an hour of my day, and no, I didn't get paid.

FRIDAY MORNING

I'd not had any work all week, it was September and there were slim pickings on the work front. I was up and raring to go early that morning, hoping for a call. It was unfortunate that it was a Friday, as the kids can usually be off the wall, but in most schools, there's golden time to look forward to … an excellent opportunity to get marking done.

The call came in at 7:05am, it was an early one but it gave me the kick start I needed. I was at the school on time, 8:10am. The school operated one of the new-fangled sign-in systems, similar to those they've just started using in doctors surgeries. I pressed the sign-in button and it asked me to put in my initial so it could check if I was in the system. I thought that was pointless as I couldn't be in the system as I'd never been before, but it looked like I was going to have to do it anyway.

'Oh, is it Carly?' a voice came from the office. I nodded. 'We've put you in the system.'

Oh, well that was rather nice of them. I put in 'C' and sure enough, there were a list of names, one of which was 'Carly Harley'. I selected it and proceeded to put in my car registration number as it requested and let it take my photo. Then, like magic, it printed me out a sticker ... I hate stickers. The never stay on, they peel off ... and the best bit, the sticker had my picture on, VISITOR in massive letters (as if a new face wasn't enough of an advert for trouble) and just underneath, 'Carly Harley,' not 'Mrs Harley' or even 'Ms Harley' because the system was incapable of knowing my marital status unless someone told it. Fantastic! As if being on supply wasn't tricky enough! On this occasion, it was not going to be easy to convince the children as I usually like to do, that my first name is actually 'Mrs' and to be a teacher your parents must name you 'Mrs' or 'Miss'.

'I'll take you down to the classroom,' said the lady in the office, and then she let me through the security doors. I couldn't get in without a fob, (and I wouldn't be receiving one) I also couldn't get out without one. We walked down a corridor, went through another security door, turned left and then turned right. 'Here's the staffroom, help yourself to tea, coffee, etcetera.' Then we went through another security door, 'Staff toilets are here, they're unisex ones as we've only got ten male members of staff working here.' (That seemed like enough to let them have their own toilet to me). Further down the corridor was yet another security door. We made another left and arrived at the classroom. 'Here we are,' she chirped as she opened the door to the messiest classroom I had ever seen.

There were papers strewn all over the sides and across the teacher's desk. In the middle of each of the children's tables were cleaning boxes with everything thrown in; screwed up bits of paper, broken pencils and three or four pencil crayons of only one colour. Next to the boxes on each table were two piles of work that had been crumpled after they'd obviously being sitting there for weeks without being stuck into their books.

'Is there a set plan to follow?' I asked. 'Or is it just, 'do your own thing?''

'The teacher's been off for five weeks now so you'll have to do your own thing. There are only twelve students in the class.'

'Oh, how lovely!' I replied excitedly.

'This year five and six class is a bit wild. You're the tenth teacher they'll have had in five weeks.' Oh dear, sounded like they were going to be a challenge. Only twelve kids?

'Were the teachers day-to-day supply or were you trying to get a long-term cover but no-one stuck?'

'Oh, we are trying to find a long term, it's just hard to find one, no-one has wanted to stay.' It certainly wasn't going to be me!

The teaching assistant arrived at 8:30am, Mrs Gladstone, and she seemed to be very nice and helpful, which was a relief. I flicked through my textbooks and found some work that could be done as one-off lessons for Maths and Literacy.

'Mrs. Gladstone, I wondered if you'd be able to photocopy these for me to use in the lessons this morning.'

'Ah, I'll do my best, but we actually have a reprographics lady and all photocopying has to be submitted to her with at least forty-eight hours notice. I'll see if she'll make the exception for you, but she is rather strict with it.'

Is it surprising that supply teachers get complexes, imagining all other school staff are out to get them?

She returned ten minutes later. 'She said if I take it to her between 9:10am and 9:13am, she'll do her best to get it done, but it's not a definite, so you'll need to think of an alternative, just in case. I am really sorry about this, I feel terrible.' Unfortunately, Mrs. Gladstone feeling terrible didn't change our situation.

'I think I'll just go and do the photocopying myself then, there's just about enough time,' I replied, trying not to let my anger bubble out at her, after all, she was trying to help.

'Oh, only Mrs. Fernley is allowed to use the photocopier, no-one else is permitted to touch it.' I could hear the fear in her voice.

'Oh, have you tried it before?' I questioned. Her eyes widened and her body quivered. 'Well?'

'Some things are best left unsaid,' and with that she left the room hurriedly.

A rather surreal atmosphere filled the room. I likened it to being on the set of a whodunit drama that was going to unravel itself after giving hundreds of subtle little hints.

There was no way I was planning an alternative as well. It was pretty hard to do something valuable with the whole class with no resources. Besides, these days it was different, not like when I was at school. Now, there has to be a least three different pieces of work for the different abilities in the class. In my school days, there was one thing for everyone and everyone did the same. Not only did I not have enough time to put three different sets of Maths questions on the board, I also didn't have enough room either, that'd be another reason why schools need more money these days, the paper.

My life was hanging on the edge until 9:10am, when I would find out whether or not I would be allowed to have my resources photocopied.

They did have one untouched desk in the classroom, the science display with books displayed attractively. I do try to link in with what they're doing when I can. In a box, they had some key words, the first one I pulled out was 'spine'.

I wrote on the board:

Good morning Beech class. On your whiteboards, see how many words you can make out of the word SPINE. You can use the letters more than once.

The bell rang and the children started trailing in noisily.

'There are instructions on the board, Beech class, sit in your normal places and get your whiteboards out.' I repeated this several times as more and more students flooded through the door.

Then, Miss Seed came into the class and smiled at me sweetly.

I minced over to find out what she wanted. 'Hi, can I help?'

She gave me a rather confused look. 'I'm Miss Seed,' she answered. 'I'm here to support Jorge.'

Just at that moment, another adult wandered in. I looked over in confusion. 'I'm Mrs. Reagan, I'm here to support Nala.'

Nala? I thought that was a cartoon lioness's name. Okay, so there were going to be three adults observing me making a hash of this and most likely thinking that they knew best. Lovely. This class couldn't be that bad, could it, with a child to adult ratio of 3:1?

Mrs Reagan hung her coat up on a hook behind the door and then locked her bag in a cupboard. In response, I glanced over at my bag and then pushed it a little more under the desk and out of the way, just in case.

'I see we've got yet another supply teacher...' Mrs Regan muttered loudly to Miss Seed.

Mrs Reagan sat with Nala and Miss Seed worked with Jorge while I wandered around the room trying to keep the rather loud noise level down with a constant 'shhhhh' as well as simultaneously pushing down the back of every chair so it was on four legs. It was like playing that game at the seaside where you have to bash the crocodile - as soon as you've done it, it creeps back up again and you're back where you started. It was certainly good exercise, darting around the large room with all the students spread out, probably to prevent them from killing each other.

Most of the children had little interest in my task, no matter how much I tried to coax them. This was a 'make out like you're their friend' kind of school, similar to my days of secondary school teaching. The kids were well beyond their years in street knowledge and the prospect of a 'prize' had very little leverage with them unless the prize was the opportunity to swipe my iPhone. It was rather tiring offering constant encouragement in an attempt to manipulate them into getting something done.

'Miss, I can't do it, it's too hard,' Kelly whined.

'You haven't made any words yet, you must be able to think of one.'

'I can't. You do it for me.'

'Well, I think that would defeat the point here,

Kelly. What word could you make with the letters N, P and I?'

'Dunno.'

'What about 'pin'?'

'Oh yeah, thanks Miss.'

I'd unwittingly fallen into her trap. 'Try another.'

'Don't wanna.'

'Come on, I'm sure you do.'

'You can't make me.'

'I bet you can't do ten in two minutes.'

'No I can't.'

My powers of persuasion and reverse psychology were failing me here. I racked my brain for alternative methods of manipulation that I'd picked up along the road. I decided that ignorance was best - it was bliss and I moved to the other side of the room.

James was hard at work, unlike the others. It seemed like he was quite a bright boy and willing too. He had sixteen words on his board. I glanced down his list:

NIP
PIN
PINE
SIN
NIPS
PINS
SPIN
IN
INN
SIP
PENS
PEN
IS
PENIS

'Er, rub THAT word off please!' I demanded. Although it *was* the longest word he'd come up with and it *did* use the correct letters.

'Which word?' he said grinning, coaxing me to say it.

'THAT word,' I insisted, pointing at it.

'You mean penis?' he sang gleefully.

'Yes I do, remove it!'

'But it's a real word. All boys have one.'

'Yes I know it is and I know they do but...'

'How do you know, Miss?' Kelly piped up, 'Have you seen one?'

'Now that's enough!' I bawled, 'There'll be no more of this talk.'

The class went silent for a second or two and they all looked down at their work as if contemplating whether or not to proceed with it.

James rubbed it off clumsily with attitude and muttered under his breath, 'We use that word in sex education ALL THE TIME.'

I thought that this was a good cue to do the register. 'Kelly-Ann-Rosybella.'

'Grr... it's just Kelly.'

'Okay, but it says here ... never mind. Jorge.'

'Here Mrs er...'

'Harley,' whispered Miss Seed in his ear.

'Here, Mrs Highley,' shouted Jorge. I glanced up at him in despair, as if peering over my imaginary glasses.

'Roxanna.'

Silence.

'Roxanna.' A slight girl tiptoed into the room and sat down. I assumed she must have been Roxanna. 'Roxanna,' I repeated, looking at her.

'Miss, she doesn't speak any English,' Kelly

announced.

I continued, 'James.'

'Here,' he said in an almost inaudible grunt.

'Abel.'

'I'm not called Abel, it's Atif.'

'Erm ... okay, I'll try to remember that. Apple.'

'Here.'

'Serish.' The class started giggling. I looked up as my eyes narrowed, I was not in the mood for any more messing. The niceties had left me, already! 'What's the problem?'

'It's Sarish, not Serish.'

'It says Serish here.'

'Yes that's how it's spelt, but it's not how you say it.'

'Sarish.'

'Here.'

'Nala.'

'Here.'

'Harley.'

'Here, Mrs Harley.'

'Harley, you have such a lovely name. I personally think it's the best name in the class,' I chirped knowingly. It occurred to me that she was three sheets to the wind as she gave me that 'I have no idea what you're going on about' kind of stare.

'Peter.'

'Here, Mrs Harley.' I was rather surprised to hear a female voice reply.

A stocky boy barged through the classroom door with his 'big man walk' and slumped down on a chair before putting his head in his hands, probably to go to sleep. I could probably predict the first letter of his name.

'Amethyst.' Really? Amethyst?!

'It's Amethyst-Gemstone. It does say it on the register. I like to be called by my proper, full name,' she insisted.

'Amethyst-Gemstone it is.' I continued, 'Bradley.'

He lifted his head but stayed in his slumped position whilst he shouted loudly, 'Here Miss!' in the attempt to get himself a laugh, all the while sniggering at his own wonderful humour. Yes, his name began with 'B'.

It was 9:05am and I began to panic as I had not seen Mrs Gladstone in a while. We would be cutting it fine and my fate rested on this photocopying lark.

'Do you happen to know where Mrs. Gladstone is?' I asked Miss Seed. She was the least scary of the two, so I singled her out as my 'confident' for the day.

'She'll be in class in a few minutes, she guards the outside door until ten past.'

Oh no! This was really bad! It shortened our window of opportunity even more. What if Mrs Fernley's watch was a few minutes fast or slow compared to mine or Mrs Gladstone's? I looked at my watch again 9:06am. The classroom clock said 9:07am.

'What time do you make it on your watch?' I asked Miss Seed.

'It's 9:09am by my watch,' she offered.

Crumbs, I was in an American thriller and the world was about to end – I had to intervene. I ran over to the text books in slow motion and thrust them at Kelly.

My voice followed the same, slow motion pattern with some kind of southern American accent thrown in, 'Run, Kelly, run! Take them to Mrs Gladstone, tell her not to delay!'

Kelly grunted, dragged herself out of the seat,

pulled the text books from the table and strolled out lazily, the text books hanging loosely from her hand, trailing behind her. It was the end, I could see it, she wasn't going to make it. Best start thinking fast.

For the next three minutes, I chewed my fingernails nervously and paced back and forth, desperately trying to conjure up something to do with this dreadful class.

9:14am and in walked Mrs Gladstone, photocopied papers in hand with Kelly trailing behind. Oh, the relief.

'Right Beech class, stop and look this way please.' I waited for the class to stop talking, I waited some more, I waited some more again, 'Right year five and six, that's enough! When I'm talking, you're not talking.' I was just about to start the lesson when I could hear muttering again, it was Mrs Reagan chatting to Miss Seed. I could even hear what she was saying.

'If she thinks she's gonna get silence out of this class, she's got another thing coming. Her best bet is to just shout over the kids, see if they take anything in.'

'I can still hear muttering,' I said sternly as I looked their way.

Mrs Reagan ignored me completely as she continued. 'Fancy sharing two's with me at break time?' she asked.

Miss Seed caught my eye and motioned for Mrs Reagan to shut up. They both grinned at me sarcastically.

'Right children, today in Maths we are going to be looking at multiplying numbers by ten and one hundred.' I wrote the date and the learning objective on the board with the pen that was on the platform just under it. I drew out the place value columns with a decimal point and columns after it.

'Can I just stop you there, Mrs....' interjected Mrs

Reagan.

'Harley. What is it?' I asked.

'Well there's no point in you carrying on because we've got a visitor coming in ten minutes and we've all got to go to the hall.'

This was news to me. 'Ah, okay then. I guess we'll just play hangman for ten minutes then.' I picked up the cloth also on the platform under the whiteboard and started rubbing. Nothing. It wouldn't budge. I gave it a bit more welly but nothing happened. I started to panic, and the children started to snigger. I looked down at the pen I'd used, permanent marker.

Anxiety was beginning to set in, and I spun around in a frenzy, but I knew if I was going to survive the day then I had to ignore it and concentrate on the children. A large, deep breath.

'Right children, this is a bit unorthodox but as we have five minutes to kill, let's play the celebrity name game. I'll say a celebrities name like Justin Beiber, and then the next person has to say a celebrity's name that begins with 'B' and so on. So I've said Justin Beiber, James, you're next.'

'Bruno Mars.'

'Your turn now, Kelly.'

'Michael Owen.'

'Very good. Atif.'

'Olly Murs.'

'Brilliant. Jorge?'

'Mrs Reagan,' blurted Jorge.

'It has to be someone famous Jorge.'

'Maria Connor on Coronation Street.'

'Well Maria's not technically a celebrity is she? She's a character. Anyway, it's probably time to line up.'

The kids lined up, well, if you could call it a line, more like a dog's hind leg, and set off towards the school hall. I took Mrs Gladstone to one side to see if she could track down the caretaker to sort out the small mishap that had occurred. Hopefully, he'd be understanding.

I rushed to the front of the line where we were stuck at the first security door. I leaned back and gazed down the corridor to the back of the line to get Mrs Reagan's attention. When she'd finally stopped gassing she padded down slowly, dragging her feet all the way to open the door with her fob. Her fob gave her power over humble supply teachers and she loved every minute of it.

'Miss... are you called Carly?' asked Amethyst-Gemstone.

'I've already told you my name, it's Mrs Harley.'

'No, but your real name?'

'That is my real name.'

'But it says Carly Harley on your badge.'

'They must have made a mistake.'

'Eh? Why would they do that?'

'Strange things happen in schools.'

'Everyone,' she shouted, 'Miss' real name is Carly.'

Bradley piped up, 'Alreet Carly.' How brilliant! Just what I needed.

'That's enough of that. I expect to be called Mrs Harley.'

I led the way as we trekked along to the next security door, imagining that Mrs Reagan would have stayed two steps behind me, like any sensible adult. As I approached the door I swung round so I could step out of her way. She hadn't even turned the corner yet. I heard her voice before I clocked eyes on her. As she came around the corner with Miss Seed she looked me in the eye and then slowly trudged towards us. Thank goodness there was only one more door.

I slowed down this time, perhaps she was finding it hard to keep up as she was on the larger side and getting on a bit. I turned around at the last security door, expecting her to be no more than halfway down the line. She'd completely disappeared! I could see Miss Seed, but no Mrs Reagan.

'Miss Seed, is Mrs Reagan around that corner?' I called down the corridor.

'Oh no, she's gone back to the loo. Said she really needed it.'

'Right …. So …. well, can use your fob on this door then please so we can get to the hall?'

'Umm, no, that wouldn't be possible.'

'And why is that?'

'Well, I've left it in the classroom. I never take it around with me. We'll just have to wait for her to come back. I'm sure she won't be long.'

'Brilliant.' The sarcastic tones in my voice were extremely colourful.

There were no other classrooms amid the two security doors we were locked between so no-one could help us out. The children were loud, but thankfully they were only chatting at this stage. I feared that a longer stint in this cell could have more serious repercussions, probably for me.

We waited, then waited, and waited. After ten minutes, she still had not returned. Suddenly, James slammed Kelly up against the wall and held her by the scruff.

'Say that about my mum again and you're dead,' he yelled. I'd predicted it.

'Now, now children. Let's break this up,' I said putting my hands together in a prayerful position and placing them in between the two kids to prise them apart. I hauled James down to my end of the corridor and told Kelly to go to the other end. 'Let's just calm down.'

After two minutes everything was fine again and they were even laughing and joking with each other. All had been forgiven.

Mrs Reagan trotted in carelessly, two travel cups in hand. I couldn't believe it! She'd obviously been to the staffroom to get her and her mate a coffee while we'd been stuck here for over ten minutes. I stopped myself from calling out, 'I have a travel cup too'.

'Oh, I didn't think you'd still be here. You weren't waiting for me were you?'

'Well as you're the only one with a fob, we've had quite a job on, trying to get out!'

'Never mind, eh. I just got chatting. Mrs Fernley in reprographics has some hilarious stories to tell, she had a fifteen minute free window.' I'd been lead to believe that that woman was rushed off her feet!

She waddled down the corridor, coffee cups slowing her down even further, then handed me one to hold while she unlocked the door. That was strange, it didn't seem hot, or full. I was sure by now that we would be in lots of trouble for being so late for this visitor. We were the only class that he was coming to see.

I ushered the class in and it seemed he hadn't yet arrived, so I decided that a circle would be the best position for them to begin sitting in. The loud chatter filled the hall and the acoustics trebled the volume. I continued with my constant 'shhh' but it didn't appear to be working.

Just then, Mrs Reagan picked up the travel cups up from the bench. 'Right, I'm going to the staffroom to make Miss Seed and myself a coffee.' Off she toddled to the staffroom. Unbelievable.

Controlling the children whilst waiting for the visitor was a nightmare.

'Sit up please, James. Kelly, stop rolling on the floor, I won't tell you again. Nala, it's bad enough picking your nose, never mind eating it as well. Go get yourself a tissue.'

'But Miss, the toilets are at the other side of the security door.'

'Oh forget it! Chew away, Nala, chew away! Atif, stop poking Bradley in the ribs. Bradley, stop holding Atif in a headlock. Well done, Harley, what a wonderful example you're setting the rest of your class. You obviously want to win a prize from my box at the end of the day.'

'Er ... swot,' yelled Kelly. 'Don't even care about them rubbish prizes.' The bribes were working a treat then.

The behaviour didn't change when the deputy head entered the room. They obviously had a deep respect for her too.

'Are you the supply teacher that's covering this class?' Yes, that's my name ... supply teacher!

'Yes, that's why I'm with them.'

'Well, can I ask you what you're doing in here then?'

'We're waiting for the visitor to arrive.'

'What visitor?'

'Apparently a visitor is coming to do a session with the class.'

'No, no, there must be some kind of mistake. I'm teaching year two in here in five minutes, you'll have to go back to class.'

'Okay, but what about the visitor?'

'No, no, you've got it wrong, there's no visitor. Right Beech class, line up by the door please.'

Groans, mutters and grunts were heard as they lumbered over to the door and scratched their confused bear heads. I didn't blame them either, not only was I being messed around, which I was used to, but they were too.

'We can't actually get back to class though as we don't have a fob to get through the security doors.'

'That's okay, I'll take you back.'

She walked very fast. I skipped to keep up the pace and most of the children tried to keep up too. She opened the first door and Harley held it open for the stragglers. She opened the second door and Peter held it open, by now the class had split into two groups, the children interested in keeping up, and the children lagging behind.

'Mrs Peterson,' (that was the deputy head) called a voice from way down the corridor, 'There's a phone call for you.'

'Ah, I've been expecting that. Highly important, I must take it. Peter, come with me, I need you do to do me a very important errand.'

Almost as if in slow motion Peter let go of the door and walked away from us with Mrs Peterson. Seven of us were at one side of the security door and the remaining six were at the other side.

'Jorge!' I yelled, 'Grab the door.' His reaction was rather delayed and he reached for it as it slammed, but it was too late. In the same moment, Harley allowed Mrs Peterson and Peter though her door and then trotted down the corridor to catch up. Mrs Peterson and Peter were in the hall at the other side of the other locked security door and no, they hadn't noticed.

I peered at Miss Seed and the other children through the glass in the door. They were trapped in their bit and we were trapped in ours.

Nala was in my corridor and when she realised that she had been separated from Miss Seed and that she was stuck with a random teacher that she didn't know, she began to cry uncontrollably. As I was obviously the problem, every time I got closer to her and tried to comfort her it got worse and she bawled louder and louder. The only solace I could take from it was that perhaps her whining would trigger someone to come and find out what was going on. Usually, I would find this kind of thing highly embarrassing, as it looked like I wasn't in control of the situation, which I wasn't, but by now, I really didn't care.

Her whimpering did just the trick and Mrs Reagan trolled down the corridor, hot travel cups in hand.

'Trapped again? I only left you for a few minutes. You're not very 'in control' are you? Good job I'm here to rescue you again.' As a professional, I ignored it, I'm not saying it was easy though. I was the first back to the class where I slumped down onto the swivel computer chair, rested my elbow on the desk and dropped my head into my hands.

Just as the children were trailing into the class the bell went. They bounced up and down with excitement, did an about turn and pranced out of the room, not waiting for my dismissal, and you know what? I didn't care!

I fished in my bag for a chocolate bar. I didn't have coffee, but I did have chocolate.

I pondered over what to do in the next session. They were so high now, it was going to be really difficult to bring them back down to earth to do some learning.

I glanced over at the white board, the permanent marker was still there. I guessed I'd just go with the flow and not worry about it too much.

To get to the staff toilet I needed to get through two security doors. I had ten minutes left of playtime, so I hoped it would be enough time to get to the toilet and back. I set out in search of an adult with a magical key fob. The teacher two rooms down from me was thankfully in her room and she was on her way to the staffroom so I followed her down. That was the getting there sorted. I reached for the unisex toilet door and pushed. The stench hit me. It was pretty obvious that men were also using this toilet. There were 'dribbles' all over the floor and 'dribbles' all over the seat. I went back onto the corridor and checked the door again. It definitely said, 'Staff Toilet'. I had thought for a moment I was in the kid's one by mistake. I wiped the seat with toilet roll and hovered. I'd have to stop myself from drinking a lot of I wanted to avoid a visit in here again.

Minutes later I was out in the corridor again, willing a member of the magical key fob gang to come to my rescue. I went up to one of the doors and pressed my nose up against it. Nobody. I trotted back to the other door and pressed my nose up against that one. A person! I could see a person! And ... it was an adult. I hammered on the door frantically and he walked over.

'Can you let me through please?' I shouted through

the tiny air gap where the frame and door met.

'No can do. I'm a visitor too,' he said, showing me his badge with VISITOR on it. I don't know why they don't change it to BEWARE. 'I'll see if I can find someone though.'

'Thanks.' I only waited a few moments before he came back with another man, this guy was good.

'I've brought the caretaker.' The caretaker! Eeek!

'Are you the supply teacher in Beech class?' he rasped.

'Erm ... yes, that would be me.'

'Yeah, well you've ruined that board! It's going to take me hours to clean.'

'Yes, I'm very sorry about that. It really was an honest mistake. Might be a good idea to confiscate that permanent marker.'

He unlocked the door and growled. I ran away fearfully like a child, worrying that he might chase after me. The gentlemanly, visiting stranger held the last door open for me and I couldn't help but feel we had common ground as visitors, both strangers to be wary of. I had a friend, an accomplice.

The bell sounded and break time was over so I garbed up in my coat and gloves. You can never trust how long you'll be stood out there because, even though it's technically within your control, it's out of your control. If the little darlings can't stand still or shut up you could be stood in the cold or rain for twenty minutes and although it is the teacher's choice to do so, they force it upon you by being idiotic. I never leave it to chance.

Surprisingly, the break time staff had organised them into four neat lines. None of the other teachers appeared to have exited the building to collect their classes. This happened to me a lot, if I'm never sure if they need to be collected, so I do it anyway just in case.

I looked closely at each class. It was very confusing. There's always the worry that after a fifteen minute break, you'll forget the faces of the class you were teaching, as after all, you see thirty new ones every day. I squinted at the first line. I was sure I recognised someone in that line. No, it couldn't be my class, I didn't recognise the others, it must have been someone's brother. I studied the next line, I thought I recognised one of the children in this class too. Perhaps they had a cousin that went to another school that I've been to. My eyes began darting from line to line, why couldn't I remember which class I had? This was going to make me look a complete fool. I was going to have to bite the bullet.

'Excuse me,' I said to the adult stood next to me, 'this is going to sound really silly, but, I can't seem to work out which class is Beech class.'

'They're lined up in houses. You can go back inside, you don't need to take them in,' she chuckled. What a relief! I thought I was going mad. The first line was dismissed and they began shooting off in all different directions. I rushed back inside to save my iPhone from sticky fingers getting into class before me.

Back in class everyone sat down and it seemed to me that they were the calmest they had been all day. I wasn't sure whether to appreciate it or worry that there was a storm brewing.

'Okay Beech class, we are going to...' I started.

'Take it back!' James erupted.

Who was he talking to?

'Get lost. I'm not taking it back,' retorted Kelly from the other side of the room.

'Take it back now or I swear I'll... I'll...' Maybe he didn't know what he was going to swear.

"You'll what? I'm not scared of you,' she teased.

'Okay guys, let's talk about this sensibly,' I said, not really knowing my next move. My eyes searched frantically around the classroom for an adult to help with this but of course, four adults assigned to the room, but the rest hadn't returned from their break yet.

James got out of his seat and began walking with attitude over to Kelly.

'Oh come on now, James, let's not do anything silly. You're not going to hit her are you? She's a girl and it wouldn't look good for your street cred.'

He edged closer so I edged closer. He got within inches of her face so I started to panic and moved up behind him, hoping to intervene. He picked up her full water bottle and began walking past her. This confused me. Was he stealing it? Seconds later, he'd unscrewed the top, turned around and poured the lot over her head!

The whole class, including me, was stunned. I didn't really know where to put myself.

'Right James, out.' I really needed another adult to help me sort this issue but I wasn't that privileged.

'No, I'm not going,' he spat. Great! What now?

'Harley, could you go to the office please.' I gave her the red card hung on the wall that had to be used for emergencies. I wasn't sure how long she'd actually be because it wasn't as if she could actually get to the office. Once Harley had left the room, James decided he'd leave too. Typical.

There were still droplets of water falling from Kelly's hair and on to the table as most of the class surrounded her, constantly asking her if she was okay.

'Take your jumper off, Kelly, it's soaked. Is your t-shirt underneath wet too?'

'I'm not taking it off, I'm self-conscious about myself.'

'Well you can't sit in wet clothes. Change into your PE top.'

'I don't have a PE top.' This was just getting better.

Harley re-appeared with Miss Seed. She'd found her roaming the corridor aimlessly on her way back from the staffroom and helped her to find the head teacher, who was now outside the room with James.

I went to tell her what had happened. She wasn't interested at that stage in what I had to say.

'Aww, James darling, what's the matter? This isn't like you getting involved in silly things. What's happened to make you like this?'

'Excuse me,' I began, to give the head teacher a fuller picture.'

She glared at me. 'I'll find out your side of the story later!' Was she really implying....?

I persisted, 'Erm, Miss, I think Kelly needs to...'

'I'm busy here at the moment, as I've just said, I'll find out what *you* have to say afterwards.'

Personally, I was thinking that it might have been more important that Kelly was found some dry clothes, but I'm only a lowly supply teacher, what do I know?

Ten minutes of mollycoddling proceeded while I tried to keep order in the classroom. Then it was our turn to tell our version of events. She'd sent for a learning mentor to sit with James as we, apparently, just couldn't possibly understand what he was going through at this difficult time ... that was because as usual, we were not allowed to know.

The door crashed open and James stormed into the classroom, the learning mentor scuttling behind. He headed straight for the stock cupboard, slammed the door behind him in the face of the learning mentor and wedged the chair in there under the handle to lock himself in. He just sat there alone in the dark.

'James,' Miss Cox, the learning mentor called sweetly. 'Open the door, James, we just want to talk.'

'I'm not coming out! You'll blame it all on me and she'll get away with it like she always does. Go away, I'm staying put.' She'll get away with it? She wasn't the one who poured water over someone.

'Come on, James.'

'No, that teacher's got it in for me. She hates me. She'll take Kelly's side.' Oh really? I'd hardly spoken to him, certainly not about this. A dirty tactic to get his own way that the staff drunk it all in. There was so much that could be observed on supply. Staff and pupils usually feel sorry for us, believing that we just 'haven't quite made it', but in all honesty, we own a greater understanding for school dynamics and could point out the good and bad things in any given educational establishment in only a few hours.

'Right Beech class, collect all of your things,' demanded the head, 'I want everyone out of this room!'

'What?'

'Go to the ICT suite, get everything you'll need and don't expect to be allowed back in before lunch.'

I grabbed my bag, coat, textbooks, iPhone, everything. I was leaving nothing to chance, or sticky fingers.

And then there were nine. The children had been instructed by another teacher to go on an educational website that the school had signed up to. It was 11:05am and we had an hour and ten minutes to kill.

After fifteen minutes or so, the kids started to get bored.

'Miss...' whined Amethyst-Gemstone.

'What is it, Amethyst-Gemstone?'

'I'm bored, Miss. I don't wanna do it, Miss. Can I go on something else, Miss?'

'No, Amethyst-Gemstone, I'm afraid you can't, Amethyst Gemstone, we've had our orders, Amethyst-Gemstone, and it's to stay on this.'

'Can't we play games, Miss?'

'Yes, Amethyst-Gemstone, you can play games on the website that we've been told to go on.'

'Awwww you're so boring, Miss.'

'I know that, Amethyst-Gemstone, and I like it that way.'

'Miss, can you stop saying my name in every sentence?'

'Amethyst-Gemstone, can you stop saying mine?'

'Eh?'

At that point I figured it was best to walk off to the other side of the classroom, to watch the other kids shut down the games websites they shouldn't have been on as soon as they thought that I was looking. What they always fail to realise is that, just because I'm an adult, that doesn't mean I'm a dinosaur. I'm only twenty-eight and I was brought up with computers just like them and I've been using the internet since before they were born. They'll swear until they're blue in the face that they didn't just click the cross button as you were meandering over to them. It couldn't possibly be something me and my friends did at school ... could it? After all, according to the kids, when I was born we probably didn't have TV's, the cane was in force and we were still using old money.

'Miss...' whined Apple. They were at it again!

'Yes, Apple.' It seemed so weird saying that. It was like, 'Hello Orange, how are you? Have you seen Banana today? Perhaps I'll go and see Strawberry for a smoothie, toodle pip.'

'Can I put the sound on so I can hear it?'

'Have you got some headphones?'

'I can get some from the cupboard.'

Anything to shut them up. 'Of course. In fact, why don't you hand them out to everyone?' This would kill some time and hopefully give them a renewed interest in this website that even I could see was boring. Apparently, this was what they did every ICT lesson too, they didn't learn how to use any of the programs, they just played on this website doing Maths, not ICT.

Apple ensured everyone received a pair of headphones, serving herself first to make sure she got the best ones. It's lovely to see a girl brought up with beautiful manners.

'Mrs Harley,' I heard from behind. Who could that strange, polite voice be? I spun around to have a peek. Harley.

'Yes Harley, how can I help you?'

'I can't get these headphones to work.' They were on her head at the time.

'Have you made sure that they're plugged in properly?'

'I tried that.' I checked and she had surprisingly, got

that bit right. 'Have a listen, Mrs Harley, it's all crackly.' She handed me the headphones and I took hold of them hesitantly. I was just raising them above my head when I spotted something running across the bridge. I looked closely and it raced to the other side and onto my hand.

'Arrrgggh!' came the highest pitched scream you've ever heard from as I dropped the headphones on the floor and shook my hand with vigour.

'What's the matter, Mrs Harley?' asked Harley.

'Oh nothing, I, um, just thought I saw something.' I bent down to retrieve the headphones and inspected them closely. The 'creature' had gone. 'Anyway,' I said, peering over and taking a good look at her head, 'where were we?'

'You were going to listen to the crackling.'

'Oh yes, I think they're probably just rubbish, I mean, er, broken. Um, just go get another pair.' At that point, I noticed that her hair was teeming with lice, taking it in turns to slide down the strands of hair, onto her shoulders and then walk back up, a little bit like children on the helter-skelter at a fairground. 'On second thoughts, I think it's the computer. It's probably best if you just don't listen to the sound.'

Fearing the worst, I proceeded to wander around the classroom, peering onto all the scalps as I passed. Thankfully, I didn't spot any other children with friends nesting in their hair. Nevertheless, I began with the subtle little itches all over my scalp, causing me to scratch uncontrollably every time it occurred. It must have looked like I'd suddenly developed some kind of Tourette's.

A loud banging noise was heard coming from the other side of the door. It was Peter. I smiled at her sweetly, unable to open the door to let her in. It was only then that it occurred to me the bother we'd be in if there was a fire. I hoped that the doors would automatically unlock in the event of it, but if that didn't happen, we'd have been screwed. Fortunately, Miss Seed was about ten steps behind her, this time, with her magical key fob. I've no idea to what we owed the pleasure, but Miss Seed had decided that we were now worth bothering with and she stayed for the rest of the lesson. At least I was no longer adult-less with no way to escape.

Shortly after, there was another loud bang on the door, this time it was Kelly sporting her tracksuit bottoms and a hooded top. Her Dad had been called and he'd brought a dry change of clothes into school for her. The rest of the class had a good old moan about Kelly being allowed to wear non-uniform and how they wanted to wear their 'home clothes' too.

Finally, the learning mentor returned James to the class. I had thought that it was to apologise to Kelly and myself. However, he walked straight to the other side of the room and sat down at a computer. I looked over at the learning mentor in confusion, who was still standing in the doorway. What a merry dance he's taking her on, I thought. Walking off from her and sitting at a computer after what he's done, especially after stealing the amount of staff time from the other children that he's required this morning, due to being less than reasonable. Minutes passed and she was still there, James had now logged on. By this point, I was pretty bewildered. It couldn't be possible that she'd actually brought him back to class ... could it?

'Is James supposed to be in here with me now then?' I called over to the learning mentor. She responded with a single nod. So I was expected to accept him back with no qualms then and just ignore the fact that he was out of control. I suppose I should have been thankful that we were able to get back into the classroom again.

There were fifteen minutes remaining until lunchtime and the kids were whining about their boredom more than ever. I just wanted to get to lunch time as quickly as possible.

'Okay children, you may have free choosing for the last fifteen minutes before lunch.'

The children cheered loudly in response. I slumped in a corner and waited for the bell to ring.

FRIDAY AFTERNOON

Although it may seem like I'm being ungrateful, hour long lunchtimes can be such a drag when there's not even the slightest spot of marking to do.

After I'd checked my e-mails, text a few people, caught up with social networking, had a nosy at the textbooks to see if there was any I didn't have and emptied my travel cup of the remaining cold coffee, I sank into the swivel computer chair and rested my chin on my hand that was being supported by my elbow. It had only been five minutes. It was time to open the lunchbox. Just as I was reaching into my bag, I could hear a rowdy racket tumbling through the outside doors. I sat up in confusion and then turned my focus to outside. It was raining cats and dogs.

As a rule, I never visit the staffroom to engage in all the mindless small talk, even if that means sitting in with the class and the dinner lady on a wet lunchtime while I graze over my lunch and continue marking books. This class, however, were one of a kind, and I wanted, no, needed, separation from the children.

Before they raided my sanctuary, I grabbed my bag and headed for the staffroom. I waited at the first security door for a few minutes before someone came to my rescue. Luckily for me they were going to the staffroom too.

Once there, it was rather empty. I imagined most of the teachers would be trailing in as the children poured into their rooms. I was actually hoping that the staffroom would be slightly warmer than all the other places in the school. That's something else you can never predict on supply, how warm it will be. It wasn't warmer. This school was certainly one of the colder ones I'd been to and I'd forgotten my back-up cardigan.

I thought back to the comment that the lady from the office had made earlier, 'Help yourself to tea and coffee'. It really was out of character for me to consider it, as usually the staff have to pay subs and they get pretty annoyed when a scrounger supply teacher comes and steals all their milk, especially if supply teachers are a regular occurrence, which I assumed would be the case in this school as most teachers would be going off sick with 'stress' at some point because of the *challenging* children. I could have said horrible... but then it wouldn't have been fair on the nice kids. Apparently it's alright to lumber someone like Harley with the title 'challenging' even though she wasn't, but not James with the term 'horrible' even though he was.) Anyway, back to tea, coffee and milk - it's like the other staff reckon we 'supply teachers' bring our cereal with us every morning and fill a bowl with their precious milk.

'Oh no, we are out of milk,' said one teacher to the other at the end of one break time.

'I saw the supply teacher with cereal earlier,' the

other replied.

They look at each other and agree, 'She must have stolen it, there's no other explanation!'

Back to the point, it was really cold and I just decided that today would be the exception to the rule and these people would just have to let me have a free spoonful of coffee and a splash of milk. If they were really desperate then I could always see if I could copper together twenty pence to keep them happy.

I gingerly crept over to the cupboard and opened it. No, cups were not in that one. I searched through them all, opening the doors, carefully and quietly, hoping not to attract too much attention. I felt like I was rifling through a stranger's drawers. I located the coffee first and then the cups.

I'm quite partial to a rather hot, strong, steaming cup of Joe, so when I spotted the porcelain mug with straight, parallel sides, I singled it out as the cup for me. It even said on it 'Teaching Sucks', so it was very apt for this particular day too. I made my coffee with a heaped teaspoon and then reclined back into one of the low bucket chairs, both hands hugging the mug that I held close to my lips as I sipped the steaming coffee. Sippity, sip, sip.

Moments later, I'd slipped into another surreal dimension, where I appeared to be re-enacting 'Goldilocks and the Three Bears'.

A large, burly woman thundered into the room, her shoulders were hunched and her arms hung from them like an orangutan with knuckles trailing on the floor. She flung open the cupboard I'd collected the cup from and a loud clatter was heard as she searched impatiently.

'Who's been drinking out of my cup?!' she bawled.

Boy, she was scary. I sank down into the uncomfortable bucket chair a little further and now I was using my hands to cover as much of the cup as possible ... surely, it had to be me. No one would intentionally cross this woman.

She turned towards me and snorted, like a bull ready for the charge. I curled up in my seat. 'And who is sitting in my chair?!' she bellowed as she charged over and towered above me while I cowered uncontrollably.

'Erm, I guess that would be me, but I honestly didn't realise it was your cup or your seat. I am very sorry. I'll, er, get up.' I slid off the chair trying to get away from her but she followed. She growled as her eyes narrowed, she wanted more. 'And I'll, er, I'll wash this cup ... and ... and then you can use it.' A nervous laugh followed and it was met with another evil stare. What a horrible woman!

I filled the washing-up bowl with washing-up liquid and warm water and frantically scrubbed away, wiping away every trace of coffee and drained it on the side. I stalked backwards, edging away from her slowly and lowered myself onto one of the hard plastic chairs in the corner that everyone obviously avoided sitting on.

Highly embarrassed, I began 'playing' on my phone, although I wasn't, I was just scrolling back and forth, trying to look like I was popular and had something to do.

Just as I thought the moment had bubbled over and the spectators had begun to forget about it, a pair of scruffy, biker boots appeared in front of my bowed head. My eyes followed the trunk of her broad body and there she was again, towering above and breathing teacher breath at me.

'This tea tastes of coffee. I hate coffee. There has

never been a single grain of coffee, ground or instant that has seen the inside of this cup. You have ruined a sacred receptacle!' she spat. It seriously was like being in the same room as Miss Trunchbull.

I couldn't decide which was more shocking, the fact that she had spoken to me in that way or that the rest of the staff had allowed her to it. I picked up my bag and half eaten sandwich and headed to the car park. The rest of my lunch time was spent in the peaceful sanctuary of my car.

I trudged back to class ten minutes early as my phone battery was beginning to run low because I'd messed around with it that much amidst my boredom. I could hear the sound of mess as I approached the classroom. Through the open doorway, much was visible. Paper snowballs were being thrown with force from one side of the classroom and then back again. The chairs and tables had been moved and turned on their sides to create a 'barrier' right down the middle of the room. I was beginning to wonder if the lunch time supervisor had organised this as she seemed to be laughing along with the antics as she sat on a table at the front of the class, but even I could see, the 'teams' had been unfairly cast.

I slipped into the room unnoticed and took a few minutes respite in the stock cupboard that James had barricaded himself in earlier. Twinkling up above, like a jewel glowing in Aladdin's cave, was a tin of chocolates. I reached up and lifted it down. Before opening, I prepared myself for the possibility that it was just a useful tin, the chocolates long gone in a distant past Christmas. I popped it open and peeked inside. Pretty colours glinting in the shaft of light seeping through the crack in the door. I lifted the lid a little more and breathed in. Chocolates. I unwrapped two of the strawberry flavoured ones and deposited them into my mouth, whole. The sweet, scintillating flavours transported me to another land for all of twenty seconds until they'd dissolved completely. I was about to indulge in another when I heard the bell. I looked at my watch, 13:15, I let out a huge sigh of disappointment, replaced the tin of chocolates and made my way to the front of the class.

After the register, there were twenty minutes to kill until the Friday afternoon assembly. This was the perfect opportunity to get the classroom back to a relative state of normal. The rowdy bunch were somewhat reluctant and had to be instructed in every task.

'There are still paper snowballs all over the floor and they need picking up. What about this table? It needs to go back where it belongs. Kelly, collect all the pencils that are on the floor, Harley, you're in charge of putting the chairs back. I need all these bits of paper in the recycling bin, Apple. James, Jorge, bring that table here.' I was a hard task master but it was the only way to get anything done, aside from doing it all myself. By the time we'd finished, it definitely looked better than it had first thing in the morning. Hopefully, the powers that be would recognise that.

We followed Mrs Gladstone to the Friday Celebration assembly, who was on strict instructions not to wander off, leaving us stranded in the corridor.

Finally, we arrived at the hall, this time for a reason and there were other children and teachers there too, including the Trunchbull. It appeared that she was taking the assembly.

Beech class sat rather sensibly in their usual place and I found myself a seat on an uncomfortable, bony bench at the back. The Trunchbull called Mrs Gladstone over and had a word in her ear whilst glaring at me. Mrs Gladstone, obviously terrified, shook her head and then scurried over to a bench at the side. That's when she shot me the guilty look. It looked ominous, something was on its way.

'Good Afternoon, children, and welcome to our Friday Celebration assembly. The first award we're going to have is writer of the week.' She worked her way through every class starting with year one, right the way through to year five. 'Beech class. I don't have a certificate here for you. Your teacher obviously hasn't bothered to do one.' The children, staff and parents looked my way and I gave them a surprised, embarrassed look in return. 'So Miss......... hello, your name?'

'Er... Mrs Harley.'

'Miss Harley, who is the writer of the week in your class then?' Seriously?! For a start I'm a MRS, and more importantly, they weren't my class and I'd just met them. I'd not even done any writing with them.

'Erm .... well, erm.' I looked to Mrs Gladstone for help and she shrugged her shoulders at me apologetically.

'Well, spit it out!'

'Er...' I blurted the first name that popped into my head, 'Harley.'

'Yes, and what is it for?'

'Writer of the week, like you said.'

'Well what has she done in Literacy this week to deserve writer of the week?!' Was this some kind of sick joke where camera men were going to jump out at me and tell me I'd be fooled on camera? Appeared not.

'Well, er, she thought of some good words that she made out of the word 'spine'.'

'Right ... sounds extremely challenging. Harley, what words did you think of?' So this was an on the spot test to see if I'd made it up. None of the other teachers had been tested.

'Well, I only thought of three.'

'Only three?'

'Yes, they were pen, pin and spin, but James thought of a five letter word,' Harley replied unwittingly. I leaned forward to try and get Harley's attention to prevent this from blowing up in my face again.

'And what word was that? Spine?' and she chuckled at her own joke.

'No, it was penis.' The teachers, parents and children all gasped and turned their heads to look at me, like synchronised owls. I lifted my hand to my forehead, boiling. Cheeks, boiling. I just wanted to be out of there.

'Well that's obviously a serious issue that I'll take up with you later, Miss.....?'

'Harley. Mrs.'

She went on announce the mathematicians of the week for each class. I racked my brain for the slightest hint of Maths I'd witnessed that day so I could think of somebody, ready. She eventually got around to Beech class.

'Beech class, I think it's probably best if we leave your mathematician of the week certificate. If we're not careful, we might find out that you've been spending the day doing sums like two add one.' Ooh, she was cruel. Everything she said had to be cruel. So that was it, I wasn't to be trusted now she'd humiliated me in front of the whole school and parents, probably in case I challenged her. I was no use to her anymore.

She garbled on through certificate after certificate. There were so many, one for a tidy classroom, one for attendance, one for a thoughtful person, one for an all rounder, one for the most house points, one for the best litter picker, one for the star of the week, one for the star of the day, one for the star of the month. Oh, and it went on and on and on and on. I couldn't even think of anything to entertain myself either.

Just as I could feel my eyes closing and falling backwards off the bench was imminent, a classic piece of entertainment occurred that really brightened my day.

One of the year one children sat on the front row had a small 'mishap'. Unfortunately, he had a cold and he sneezed a very big sneeze. He'd even put his hand in front of his mouth, how polite. There was, however, a problem with that though. He didn't have a tissue at the time and so now there was a lot of snot all over his hand. He looked down at it and pulled a disgusted face and then looked around for somewhere to wipe it. At that moment, the Trunchbull, who hadn't noticed, moved just in front of him, to hand a certificate to one of the year five children. Just as the Trunchbull leaned over him and reached out her hand to shake the hand of the year five girl's, the boy sat on the front row stole his opportunity and wiped his hand down the Trunchbull's tights, from knee to ankle. I gasped, afraid that the Trunchbull would scar him for life or worse, eat him. She had noticed that he'd touched her, she hadn't noticed the snot.

'Adam dear, it's interesting that you wish to stroke my legs, but it's not something we do in polite company so please refrain from doing so again.' Did she think that he had any idea what she was going on about? Perhaps she thought it was for the entertainment of the parents? It was unlikely that they understood either. Anyhow, at least I could smirk about the fact that she had snot all over her tights to keep me going until we finally got to the end.

An amazing thing then happened. Nala told me she felt sick. Now, usually, I would try to string it out and say something like, 'Get yourself a drink of water and see how you feel in fifteen minutes' but not today. I was elated at the prospect of leaving this assembly that had now gone on for almost an hour.

I waited outside the girls toilets for her and then we climbed the stairs back to the classroom.

'Have you been sick?'

'No, nothing would come up.'

'Try drinking some water, it might make you feel better.'

Nala sipped the water from her water bottle and we both sat there quietly, enjoying the silent company. Ten minutes later, the noise rambled in along with Beech class.

'Aww, you've got to go to the headteacher's office at the end of the day,' leered Bradley. What? What was he on about?

'Pardon?'

'You've got to go to see the headteacher, you're in trouble,' he sang. Mrs Gladstone had walked in on the tail end of his comment. I looked at her with wide, pleading eyes.

'No Mrs Harley, you don't have to go to see the headteacher. Miss Dunstel (the Trunchbull) just made a passing comment to the whole school that perhaps it would be a good idea.'

'Ah, I see. And, may I ask you? Why has that woman still got a job?' The only response I got was a shrug of the shoulders.

There was half an hour left until the end of the day and apparently this school didn't do golden time, probably because none of them deserved it. Luckily for Beech class, they did now. I thought back across the day and evaluated whether or not they deserved the free time to play. I concluded that they certainly didn't, but to make life easy on a Friday afternoon we were going to do it anyway!

The kids rifled through the wet playtime cupboard that consisted of two games with half of the stuff missing whilst I meandered over to the stock cupboard to get a chocolate fix. This time I went for a milk chocolate one with hazelnut inside. I'd just popped it inside my mouth when I could hear my name being called. I chewed hastily and made my way out.

'Miss,' whined Kelly, she was good at that, 'Nala feels sick again. What are you eating?'

'Me? I'm not eating.'

'Yes you are, I can tell.' She leaned in towards me and I held my lips together as tightly as I could. 'Smells like chocolate. That's not fair. Can we have one?' I thought for a moment. I could give in and have peace but lose the precious chocolates or I could resist, keep the chocolates for myself but in turn probably create a bigger problem for myself. I'd never be visiting this school again, well, at least not while the Trunchbull was around, so there'd be no harm in raiding a few chocolates.

'Hmmm ... ok then. I suppose so, but you must make sure you give everyone just one, we can't eat them all.'

'Yes of course Miss, I'll be in charge.'

I reached for the chocolate tin, hugged them close for a second and then, not before hesitating, handed them to Kelly. Within three minutes the lot had gone! The greedy pigs had scoffed every last chocolate, even the toffee ones that I thought nobody liked. They hadn't even saved me one. It was a good job I didn't fancy returning.

'Miss, I feel really sick now!' shouted Nala.

'Did you eat a chocolate?'

'Yeah, I had ten.'

'Why did you eat them if you weren't feeling well?'

'I thought I felt better.'

I hurried over to her. 'Right, I think you need to go to the toilets, get it all out. We'll be going home in ten minutes anyway.' It was 2:55pm.

'Alright Miss...' she said, followed by projectile vomit that landed all over my half-curled-off visitors sticker and my dress. Brilliant!

Mrs Gladstone sorted out the dismissals while I was in the toilet trying to get vomit out of my clothes. Completely out of character, I waited at the exit for someone with a magical key fob at 3:15pm and then left the building, never to step foot in it again.

IT WAS A MONDAY

It was a Monday and it was snowing. For teachers, snow is more exciting than it was when you were a child. There's an inner hope that is deep rooted, a small chance that the school day will GET CANCELLED! Even as a supply teacher, knowing that not working will mean not getting paid, there's still an overwhelming attraction to staring out of the window at the white stuff all day whilst sipping hot chocolate and tomato soup (not at the same time) and watching a film you recorded off the TV at Christmas three years ago that you never got around to watching.

On this particular morning, the snow had started falling at around 5:30am and the flakes were quite big. Traffic was moving and it hadn't really stuck on the main routes very much. The call came in at 6:30am, I hadn't even got up by then. I jumped out of bed and rushed to get ready as fast as I could, building my stress levels as per usual. The school was fifteen miles away so I'd have to set off early. Why they hadn't called someone nearer in the circumstances was baffling.

Traffic was moving moderately all the way there although the snow continued to fall in large, white clumps. Every couple of miles I phoned the agency on loud speaker.

'The flakes are falling quite heavily now. Are you sure the school is still open?'

'Yes we're sure. They are determined to be open.'

'Okay, I'll keep going. Let me know if you hear different as I'm going to be a long way from home.'

'As soon as we know, we'll call you.'

I trundled along at fifteen miles per hour. I was secretly hoping they'd tell me to turn back, there were so many things I could have been doing. I phoned again. 'You're definitely sure they're still open? I've just heard on the radio that the nearby primary school is closed.'

'Honestly Carly, they're still open. They won't close, they never close for snow.'

'Okay, I'm just checking.'

I arrived at school fifteen minutes before the registration bell, so it had taken me over an hour to get there. I was a regular visitor so I smiled at the receptionist and greeted the office staff as I signed in.

'You might as well go home, we're closing the school. Some of the staff can't get in.'

'Oh, and how many miles away do they live?'

'About five miles down the road.' My face turned scarlet. I'd travelled all this way for nothing. I knew the protocol too, not getting paid despite travelling thirty miles in total.

I barged my way into the hall where they were dismissing the school children and began mucking in with the other teachers. You're probably thinking that was rather cheeky, and it was, but I wasn't going to have travelled fifteen miles for no reason and I was going to fight to be paid so I thought I'd better look like I was doing some work.

About forty-five minutes after that, the children had all gone and I began the long commute back home.

The agency told me that they'd do their best to get the school to pay me for half a day but that it would be unlikely. In the end, I did get half a day's pay for a full day that had been booked so I guess that was some kind of result.

ANOTHER MONDAY MORNING

Before the weekend I'd received a text about going to Wheatcrop School. I'd been to this school before and so I responded to confirm that I would be able to take the assignment on the Monday.

Monday came around I made my way to Wheatcrop Primary school, without the aid of my satellite navigation, as I knew where it was, only four miles away. I parked my car in the car park and signed in.

Once in the school I was met by several confused faces. In fact, more than one member of staff asked if they could help me, which was unusual. I explained to them that I was covering year three. Apparently I wasn't. I'm going to get sent home again, I thought.

'Are you sure it's not Wheatcrop Juniors that you're supposed to be going to? It's happened lots of times before.' I'd been to Wheatcrop Juniors previously, but it hadn't occurred to me that I should be going there because the text would have said Juniors, wouldn't it? I got my phone out to check the text. It didn't say Juniors, it didn't say Primary, but it did have a postcode … and looking at that, it was likely to be Wheatcrop Juniors. Oh great!

I dashed back out to the car and phoned the agency. There had been a mix up, I was now supposed to be at a school five miles away and it was 8:20am. Thankfully, we mutually took the blame between us. Why did it always happen to me?

Back in the car, I rushed across town frantically to the other school, hoping I'd make it before the registration bell went. 8:35am and I'd arrived. I dashed into the reception and signed in for the second time that morning. If I hurried to the classroom, I'd make it in there before the children did.

The children trolled in at 8:50am and I strode around the classroom, ensuring that they were reading books, or at least looking like they were. You can never actually tell if they've perfected the art of page staring or not.

I was rather unnerved in this class, as by now, there were several sets of busy-bodying parents in the room with us. It's not something I'm too familiar with, clinging on for dear life to key stage two (formally known as the juniors). I reminded myself that this was year three, and it wasn't that long ago since they were in key stage one (the infants), but technically, it had been a long time, it was July.

'Come on, Johnny, put your pencil case in your tray. Don't forget your lunch box has to go on the trolley outside.' Johnny's mum was all over him. How was he ever going to learn to stand on his own two feet with her propping him up all the time? Next, she had me in her sights. She marched over, purposefully. 'I know you're not their actual teacher, but I just wanted to let you know that it's homework day today. You'll need to collect the homework in from all the class and give them some more homework, two sheets for English and two sheets for Maths.'

'Right, ok. Well, thank you for letting me know. I'll take it up with the teaching assistant when she comes in, but it might not run as it usually does.'

'Well, I really would like him to have homework tonight.'

'I'll see what I can do, but I'm not promising anything.' Amazing how some parents think that they are the boss of the 'free childcare' system that the government pays for. Could you imagine having thirty bosses all demanding something different?

Just as I thought that this difficult situation was over I was approached by another parent.

"Ere, Mrs. I just thought I'd tell ya that Mercedes hant done her homework. It wa' too hard. I cudn't do it, it wa' too hard for me so I don't know 'ow you expect 'er to do it. I know you don't know 'er but she's not brainy, (and then she attempted a loud whisper) she's a lil bit dim ya know, like me. 'Er dad, he's the clever un. He's got a job an' everythin'. He works at corner shop down road.'

'Erm...' Why was it some parents had to talk their children into an ambitious-less life? And whether or not this parent was clever or, how she put it, dim, she didn't know when to stop talking or when she had moved onto a completely unrelated issue. 'I'll just leave a note for the teacher. It wouldn't be fair for me to decide what to do as it's not my class.'

'Oh, well, alright then. So we'll just leave it shall we?'

'Yes, I think that would be best.'

At last the adults had left the room. I opened the register and had a quick glance down. No way! It appeared that all the parents in the class must have been good friends at the time the children were born. I wasn't really sure how I was going to do the register without giggling.

'Good morning, Caprice.'
'Good morning, Mrs Harley.'
'Good morning, Mercedes.'
'Good morning, Mrs Harley.'
'Good morning, Jensen.'
'Good morning, Mrs Harley.'
'Good morning, Harley.'
'Good morning, Mrs Harley.'
'Good morning, Violet.'
'Good morning, Mrs Harley.'
'Good morning, Dino.'
'Good morning, Mrs Harley.'
'Good morning, Sienna.'
'Good morning, Mrs Harley.'
'Good morning, Celeste.'
'Good morning, Mrs Harley.'
'Good morning, Clio.'
'Good morning, Mrs. Harley.'
'Good morning, Robin.'
'Good morning, Mrs Harley.'
'Good morning, Austin.'
'Good morning, Mrs Harley.'
'Good morning, Rocky.'
'Good morning, Mrs Harley.'
'Good morning, Ford.'
'Good morning, Mrs Harley.' By this point, I was

really expecting the teaching assistant to be called Hyundai or something. Perhaps the year four class focused on something different, like electrical appliances. I could imagine kids with names like Kenwood, Philips, Hitachi, Toshiba and Dell. At least I felt that I could fit in with the year threes.

There were other children in the class too, kids who were not named after cars. One of them was called Roy and he dashed over to me as I was dutifully collecting the homework as instructed by one of the parent bosses.

'Why are you out of your seat, Roy?'

'Well I just needed to tell you this one thing.'

'Well you need to sit down and put your hand up.' He gave me a blank stare, almost like he couldn't compute what I'd said. 'Sit down, Roy.'

'But I just need to tell you...'

'Go and sit down, put your hand up and I'll come over to you.' He backed away, utterly confused.

Eventually, I got around to Roy.

'Miss, I haven't done my homework, but, but, but it's okay, because my mum said I can do it at break time.'

'Did she now? And is your mum coming in to supervise you doing your homework at break time?'

'Eh? Why would my mum come in to school?'

'Well you can't be left in the classroom on your own, so who will be staying with you?'

'You, of course!'

'Well perhaps I actually want a break at break time. Suppose I need to go to the toilet.' That comment was met by Roy pulling his head back and screwing his eyes up in deep thought. I would have loved to have known what was going through his mind, but I could give it a guess. 'I don't get it, this teacher says she goes to the toilet. Next she'll tell us that she eats lunch too like a human being and that she lives in a house. Yeah right, she can pull the other one, we all know teachers are aliens.'

'When should I do it then?'

'Roy, the clue is in the word, *home*work.'

Just before it was time to line up for assembly, I glanced around the room at the children. It seemed we had an extra one. I studied his face, trying to recall his name. I couldn't think of it and it was because I hadn't learnt it.

'Have you just slipped in? I don't remember learning your name.'

'I've just got here. I've signed in at the office.'

'Ah, ok, and what's your name then?'

'Byron,' he said with a huge grin on his face. He was rather endearing. I could tell he'd be one of those cheeky ones that you can have a bit of fun with and can't help but like.

'Ah, Byron. You know, I think there's something about Byron's, or maybe it's just boys whose names begin with 'B'.'

His face lit up and he pulled the cheekiest grin, 'Yep, 'B' for Bad Boy!' and then he giggled. He made me giggle too.

Mercedes was pretty sensible, despite the unfortunate name, and so it was her who led the line to assembly. Snaking our way through the library, we approached a traffic jam. It was quite a large school and there were two assemblies that would happen simultaneously, I assumed it would be split into key stage one and key stage two. I moved to the front of the line and lead my class through one of the assembly halls, following another year three class. On arrival at the hall entrance, I spun around to check they were lined up smartly. I was surprised to find that there was not one child there that had followed me. Where on earth had they gone? Had they become stuck in traffic again? I began to get rather cross and worked up. So far, I'd had a nice day with a nice class and now they were spoiling that so early on in the day. I raced back to the other hall and looked around, expecting them to be stood there, messing around whilst waiting to get past. To my surprise, the class were sitting smartly on the floor in neat rows with their arms folded and fingers on lips. They looked at me, puzzled, and I looked at them, confused. It turned out the classes had been split into assembly halls randomly and in my stupidity, I'd just abandoned them and waltzed off to the next hall. Looking back, I was rather impressed that they'd just got on with it and sat themselves down with no problems.

I slinked down onto a bench, trying to go unnoticed, although I'm sure my blushed face gave it away. The class were still sat smartly when the assembly started. It's funny how you can have a sense of pride for the class you're with that day, even though you don't know them. You feel something if any of them receive a certificate or are praised in any way.

It was still early in the day and they all really wanted to win a prize. Ford was sat particularly smartly. It was then that I noticed his shoes. One shoe was black with laces, the other shoe was blue with velcro.

The deputy head addressed the assembly hall, 'Good morning, children.'

'Good morning, everybody,' they chorused.

'Thank you, children, I'm going to hand you straight

over to year three now for their class assembly.' Ooh good, I thought, a class assembly. Sometimes they could be really entertaining, especially if the teacher had a dramatic, creative streak and had put a lot of thought into it. We all waited. The class who were doing the assembly hadn't budged. I scoured around to see if I could identify the class. 'Year three, are you going to come and stand at the front?' Oh my word! YEAR THREE! I was in year three! Mercedes stood up hesitantly and looked around at the other children. They followed suit and they all shuffled to the front. Perhaps they knew what they were doing ... I certainly didn't. The deputy head stood to one side to let them begin.

They stood there, frozen to the spot, whispering and muttering to each other for three minutes but they didn't move.

'How do you start your assembly, year three?' asked the deputy head, trying to give them a bit of encouragement.

'No idea. To be honest, we didn't even know we were doing an assembly today, Miss,' remarked Mercedes, 'Our supply teacher didn't tell us so she probably didn't know either. She is quite nice.'

'Right, okay then, so, there'll be no year three class assembly today then. If you just sit down again year three, we'll sing some songs for the rest of the assembly.' The children shuffled back to their places and plonked down.

It occurred to me that the deputy head was not as clued up with technology as she would have liked us to think and she was unable to get the projector to stay on. There must have been a faulty connection inside. After five minutes of messing around and the children unable to resist the urge to chatter, she decided to just put the CD on anyway.

'Okay children, we can't have the words up so you'll just have to do your best and sing along anyway.' You would have thought with that statement that she would have chosen songs that they actually knew the words to. She didn't. I'm not even sure they knew the tune. The verses consisted of a dreadful, quiet din, as nobody, not even the teachers, was actually sure of the tune. During the chorus, the tunefulness improved yet everyone sang different words. It hadn't been the best time killing idea. I had loads of those, if only she'd asked me.

When the assembly finally came to a close, I was glad to get out of there. Unfortunately, she chose to play the same song on the way out, so the children could sing it wrong all over again on the way back to class.

With the children reading quietly at their desks, I finally had the time to have a chat with the teaching assistant. She was called Miss Archer and she was really gentle with the children. I sent her off with my books to do some photocopying for the lesson.

When she returned, I was listening to Celeste read and so she left them on the teacher's desk at the front. I went over to them and took out the work that she'd placed inside each of the books. When I lifted up one the books, half of the pages fell out. I glanced over to her.

'Oh yeah, sorry about that. I was photocopying the page and they just fell out.' Of course they did, silly me. I was pretty disappointed because I had thought that we'd get on well and that we could have a bit of banter, but she'd obviously pressed on the spine that much that they'd become separated from the thread. There was no way of re-attaching them. One of the things I definitely have a thing about is looking after other people's things.

The first thing I did before starting the lesson was to get my own whiteboard pen out of my bag. This was to prevent a permanent marker issue occurring again. Then the children sat in front of me on the carpet.

Robin had his hand up. 'Yes, Robin.'

'Miss, how long 'til playtime?'

'There is one hour until playtime, Robin, when the big hand gets to six again, we'll be going out to play.'

The class had been finding out all about pirates in their topic work and so their teacher wanted them to write a description of a pirate that they'd created. We went through the usual things and wrote a list of things they could describe like his clothes, hair, eyes, pets, what he likes doing etc. Then I opened it up to the floor.

'If your pirate has his own boat, you could describe that,' offered Austin.

'What an excellent suggestion, Austin, well done.'

'You could describe how clever your pirate is,' said Rocky.

'Er ... you could. I suppose that would come under describing what your pirate is good at.'

'You could say if your pirate lives in a house or not,' Jensen answered.

'Hmmm, I think the fact that he's a pirate should technically give that answer away. Anyway, is there anyone who doesn't understand what we have to do?' They all did understand and began working quietly in their 'whisper voices'. 'Well children,' (don't forget your bouncy voice) 'I am very impressed with this noise level. I think I'm going to find it very hard to choose only two children at the end of the day to give a prize to.' At which point, they stopped the talking altogether, bless them. It was like being in heaven.

'Robin had his hand up. 'Miss, how long until playtime?'

'When the big hand gets to six, Robin. There's about thirty minutes left.'

I wandered around the classroom, reading what the children had already written and underlining the really good describing words that they'd used with my green pen, not red you'll note, as that could be seen as negative and have terrible consequences, like destroying a child's life. There were some excellent pieces of work. Violet had written;

My pirate has a long, green coat. He is abowt ten pere sent.

'Violet, 'long' and 'green' are really good describing words for your pirate's coat. I'm a bit confused though, what does the second sentence mean?'

'Well, it says on the board, how clever is your pirate? He is about ten percent clever.' Absolutely brilliant! Working in school is so comical.

'Ah right, okay then,' and with that I wandered off to have a giggle and relay the conversation to Miss Archer.

I turned around to start making my way around my class again and almost tumbled on the floor after tripping over Johnny, standing directly behind me.

'Johnny, are you out of your seat?'

'Yes but, Miss...'

'Johnny ... go and sit down and put your hand up.'

'But Miss, it'll be quicker if I just tell you now.'

'It might be, but I'm not listening until you go back to your seat and put your hand up.' A very loud sigh was heard and he skulked back to his seat. I spun around again to take the long way around the class to Johnny, to make my point and almost tripped over Roy. 'Roy! What are you doing out of your seat?'

'Miss, I just wanted to tell you...'

'What have I just said to Johnny?'

'Sit in your seat and put your hand up.'

'Correct. Why would it be any different for you?'

He shrugged his shoulders and shuffled back to his seat. Just as I began walking over to Johnny, Mercedes appeared at my side. What was this? Had I turned into some kind of magnet?

'Okay year three. Let's have every one sitting down with pencils down, arms folded and looking this way.' They quickly did as I'd asked, I couldn't fault them on that. 'What are sheep well known for?'

'Being fluffy,' remarked Robin. Well, he was right wasn't he?

'They're made out of wool,' commented Clio. I'd walked right into that one.

'Hmm, I think they have wool on them, like a cat has fur, but they're not technically made out of wool. What I mean is, do you know any sayings about sheep?'

'You have to count them to go to sleep at night,' said Jensen.

'Well yes, some people do that. It's not really the answer I'm looking for though.'

'I don't count sheep at night. We don't have any. I just go to sleep,' replied Violet.

'I've got a cat,' said Byron. I ignored that one.

'Not real sheep, Violet, pretend ones in your head. Well, never mind. The thing about sheep is that they follow each other around. They follow the shepherd around.'

'What's a shepherd?' asked Dino.

'The person in charge of the sheep.'

'So, when I'm counting sheep at night, I turn into a shepherd?'

'Er ... why not ... if you really want to ... anyway, as I was saying, they follow the shepherd around. Now children, I am not a shepherd, I'm a teacher and you are not sheep, you are children, so I don't want to be followed around all the time. If you want to get my attention, put your hand up and I or Miss Archer will come to you.' Talk about the long way around it. I wished I'd never tried to use a metaphorical example.

'Mrs Harley.' It was Robin bugging me again. 'How long until playtime?'

'Five minutes until playtime, Robin.'

'Yes!' he hissed gleefully, clenching his fist.

It was 10:25am and so we quickly tidied everything away. I had Robin collect all the books for me, open at the page the children had done the work. That's a testament to either how lazy I am or how experienced I am. Take your pick.

We could hear the bell ringing faintly in the distance. The children were dismissed and I sat down to create some lovely greenery, not reddery, on year three's books. I was just about to comment on the first piece of work when the head teacher bobbed her head around the door.

'Really sorry about this, but it's your duty.' I just smiled at her knowingly, grabbed my jacket and went out into the less than sunny, cool July weather.

'Miss,' asked Johnny, doing his sheep thing as I wandered around the playground. 'Do you want to be a real teacher?'

'I am a real teacher, Johnny.'

'No, but I mean a real, real teacher, like my teacher.'

'You mean do I want to work in one school all the time and have a class?'

'Yes.'

'No I don't.'

'Why not?'

'Because I like going to lots of different schools and meeting lots of new children.'

'Don't you like us?'

'When did I say that?'

'Well you mustn't like us if you don't want to be our teacher.'

'Johnny, I don't want to be anyone's teacher. Besides, if I was your teacher, you wouldn't have your lovely teacher.'

'I don't like her. She doesn't give out prizes like you.'

'Well I haven't given any out yet, Johnny, and I know you'd feel differently if you had to see me every day. Anyway, go and find someone to play with.' For a few moments, I was left in peace.

Mercedes approached me with Celeste. 'Miss, have you got any kids?'

'I've got fifty.'

'Fifty?! Is that even possible? I don't believe you. You must be really old. You don't look it.'

'I am old.'

'How old are you then?'

'One hundred and seven.'

'Eh … you can't be! Where's your walking stick? How come you don't have loads of wrinkles?'

'It's the night cream I use.'

'Alright then ... if you're one hundred and seven, what year were you born?'

'Er ...'

'And don't even try to work it out!'

'You should never ask a lady what year she was born. Anyway, you should be running around and chasing all the boys. Bye girls.' I began walking in a different direction to escape from them.

As I was on playground duty, I had to make sure I had a politically correct snack. I'd left my chocolate biscuit in my lunchbox until lunchtime and brought out a small bag of grapes that I'd washed at home.

Austin sidled up to me. 'I like grapes Miss.'

'Oh, very good. So do I.'

'My mum won't give me grapes, she says they're a hassle.'

'Well, it is a bit of a pain to wash them and pull them off, but it's worth it.'

'She gave me a banana.'

'They're nice too.'

'Hmm ... I'm not that keen ... Can I have your grapes?' Cheeky or what!?

'As your mum sent you with a snack and I've bought my own snack from home, I think it's quite unfair of you to ask me for mine. It's not very polite is it? I hope you don't do that with the other children.'

'No I don't, but because you're giving out loads of prizes at the end of the day, I thought you might give out free food too.'

'Two prizes, Austin, two.' I was saved by the bell. I followed the lead of the other teacher out on duty who had them line up in classes ready to go in.

There were ten minutes to kill until the bus arrived

to take us swimming. I've been to quite a few different swimming baths with school children. Most are rather relaxed and friendly, this one, however, was not.

The children collected their swimming bags table by table and lined up boy, girl, boy, girl. We were taking no chances regarding public embarrassment.

Robin appeared in front of me, pretending to be a sheep again. 'Miss, how long until lunch time?'

'It's a long time until lunch time, Robin, go and line up. Now, have we all got our swimming bags?'

'Yes!' they cheered as they held them up.

We set off along the corridors, stopping every twenty steps or so to bring the noise level down again. It's amazing how the closer the children get to you as they catch up, the quieter they become. It's like having a magical remote control for a stereo system made of children. The line expanded again like a slinky, noise levels rising and then compressed again as I halted the front and the noise levels fell.

We hadn't set off with lots of time to spare and so it was likely that the bus would already be waiting as we were a few minutes late. I marched them through the playground and we waited by the security gates. Locked in. No bus.

Obviously, it was fortunate that the bus wasn't waiting as we couldn't get out anyway, but it didn't mean that we'd get back to school any later and be able to miss any more lesson time as the swimming instructors were on an extremely tight schedule. It just meant that the already short thirty minute lesson would be even shorter. It almost didn't seem worth it.

Miss Archer came toddling out with the keys for the security gate and we shuffled out onto the pavement and waited at the roadside.

Five minutes later the bus showed up. The children attempted to push past and scramble to choose the best seats at the back.

'Hang about! I'll be telling you where to sit.'

'But our teacher lets us sit where we want. We're allowed,' insisted Caprice.

'Well your teacher isn't here now, I am, so we're going to do it my way.'

Muttering and tutting was heard. Such a satisfying sound. I directed them to their seats, filling up from the front, leaving four rows empty at the back.

Robin was the last child to climb on, just in front of Miss Archer.

'Robin, where's your swimming bag?' I questioned, hoping Miss Archer had it behind her back.

'Er ... oh no, I left it in the classroom.'

'What!? You even held your swimming bag up, I saw you!'

'Yeah, but then I saw a penny on the floor and so I put my bag down and picked it up. Then I rushed because everyone had gone.'

'Well, you'll just have to sit at the side and watch, we don't have time to be waiting around.'

'Er ... sorry to interrupt, Mrs Harley,' Miss Archer cut in. 'He has missed the last three weeks of swimming because he left his kit at home and has had to stay in school. He really needs to be swimming now he's made the effort. Besides, if he's not swimming, he can't go with us. I'd have to take him back into school anyway.' So she hadn't noticed the bag and picked it up then.

'Right, fine, looks like we're waiting another ten minutes then.'

The two of them set off back into school with not as much 'rush' as I'd have encouraged.

Eight minutes later and we were on the road, after I'd marched up and down the aisle on 'fastened seatbelt' duty.

'Robin,' I shouted down the bus. 'Make sure you keep hold of that swimming bag and don't let go of it.'

Usually on the swimming bus, I like to sit quietly gazing out of the window, occasionally glancing around the bus, checking everyone is doing as they should be. It's interesting to listen to their conversations if you can hear any. Mercedes, who was sat just across from me, had other ideas.

'Miss, have you been to Buttergrain School?'

'I've been there once, only for the morning.'

'Do you know my cousin, Bentley? He's in year one.'

'I don't really do year one and I was only there for a day.'

Celeste was next, 'You know how you used to teach at big school, do you know my sister's best friend's cousin?'

'I haven't worked in secondary for a while now so I doubt it. Which school does she go to?'

'I don't know. She goes to big school.'

'There's more than one 'big school', Celeste.'

'Oh. Well she's called Chelsea Smith.'

'No I don't know her.'

'She's got blonde hair and she's taller than me.'

'I still don't know her.'

'Do you know my Dad? He works as a car fixer.' Mercedes chipped back in. That would explain the name.

'Do you mean he's a car mechanic?'

'Er ... I don't think so. He fixes cars.'

'Yes, he's a car mechanic.'

'How do you know that? Do you know him?'

'Why would I know your Dad?'

'Because you've got a car.'

'Okay girls, it's been nice chatting, but I'm just going to sit quietly for the rest of the journey. Carry on with the conversation you were having before.' Mindless chatter going around in circles. Almost as bad as the staffroom conversations.

As we approached the swimming baths, the noise level rose and I could hear a few belts unclipping.

'Keep your seatbelts on until I tell you that they can be undone.' I barked as I marched down the bus, inspecting them closely.

'When is it lunch time, Miss?' asked Robin.

'It's not yet, Robin.'

'I know, but when is it?

'Your lunch time is at twelve-thirty.'

'But how long is it until then.'

'A while.'

'But how many minutes?'

'Seventy-five minutes. Robin, why don't you just learn to tell the time and get yourself a watch?'

'We're not allowed to wear watches at school, especially on swimming days.' I gave up, shrugged my shoulders and made my way to the back of the bus. I gave Miss Archer the nod to lead off and I began checking all the seats from the very back seat. I know that no-one had been sitting there, but experience has taught me that it was worth checking anyway.

Approaching the front, a swimming bag came into view. I pondered whose bag it could be for all of about three seconds.

'Robin,' I yelled from the bottom step of the bus. 'Have you forgotten something?'

He immediately held out his hands and looked around on the floor frantically, almost implying that his bag had been stolen from him. He then looked up at me, fear in his eyes as he knew he'd done it again. Skulking over, ashamed he took hold of the swimming bag and was surprised when I didn't let go. He tugged a bit harder, to which I responded with gripping harder. He grinned at me and then started yanking.

'Is that what you do, Robin? Snatch a bag from a teacher?'

'But you won't let go of it and you're supposed to be giving it to me.'

'Perhaps you need to say something before my hand will release the bag.'

'Sorry?'

'It's a good start, but not the word that I'm looking for.'

'It's thank you, silly!' blurted Roy. I appreciated Roy's encouragement, but not the manner in which he delivered it. I concluded that the two incidents technically cancelled each other out and so I just pretended I hadn't heard him.

Miss Archer gave out a large sigh. She was annoyed that this was wasting even more time, but I wasn't about to rush things to sacrifice the basic rules for behaving in society to get there a little quicker.

Inside reception, Miss Archer signed us in and we each took a group to get changed. It was a unisex changing room as the pool was quite new and it had four group changing rooms for school groups. Just before we started to make our way to the poolside, Miss Archer pulled out some flip flops from her bag and slipped her feet into them.

'Oh, haven't you brought any flip flops?' she asked. What a stupid question!

'It would have been rather psychic of me if I had, bearing in mind that I didn't know we'd be going swimming until an hour and a half ago.'

'Oh, right. Well, anyway, if you don't have flip flops then you have to wear those blue things on your feet.' She pointed to a box full of 'blue things'. How lovely. I slipped the super cool, plastic shower caps over my shoes. I was rather baffled in regards to the point of them as they'd all been used previously and every single one sported countless holes on the bottom. Anyhow, I was fulfilling my obligation, and that made me look good, certainly not literally.

At the poolside, the children sat down in lines and waited to be instructed by the swimming teachers. One of them barged over to me.

'Have you been before?' the instructor barked.

'I've accompanied school children swimming before, but not at this swimming pool.'

'So you know the protocol for a stand back observer?'

'Well, it's been a while.'

'I can't start this lesson until you are aware of everything you must do as a stand back observer and we're already late starting. Until your name is on that dotted line, stating that you understand what is required, these children cannot do any swimming. You need to thoroughly read this five page document.' It wasn't my fault I was a supply teacher attending the swimming lesson.

'Erm ... ok, well, perhaps you should run through them quickly.'

She gave out a large sigh. 'How many children have you with you today?' Miss Archer had signed them in, she was leading this 'trip'. How many today? It was different from yesterday and the day before that and the day before that and even the day before that.

'Er ...'

'You have to know,' she snapped. 'How many boys, how many girls?! You need to find out. You need to count the number of children in the group you are assigned to in two minute intervals. We take the stand back observer responsibility very seriously. We have had bomb scares before.' She was really frightening! She continued to rant on, going on about the protocols. She spoke that passionately (that passionately that it sounded like shouting) that by the end of it I was not exactly sure what she'd said. Something about pressing an alarm if there was a bomb scare and blowing a whistle upon drowning, or was it the other way around? 'If you fail to carry out your stand back observer role after signing, we will take you to a court of law.' She was really enticing me to sign it. I signed it, hesitantly, praying that there would be no incidents in the next forty-five minutes while we were still in the building.

I followed my group to the other teaching pool, following after the scarier of the two swimming instructors.

'Sit in the observer chair,' she commanded. I cautiously walked over and did as she said and then I carefully counted the children before they got in the water. Ten boys, four girls, fourteen in total. I repeated it to myself a few times, afraid that I might forget.

The children bounced up and down, trying to warm themselves up. Once their hair was wet, it was more difficult to tell who they were let alone what sex they were. I went through their names in my head again. Ford was in my swimming group, they were the top swimming group out of the two. Ten boys, four girls, fourteen in total.

'To start with we're going to do some push and stretches,' said the swimming instructor. She started giving them numbers, one to four. Hang on ... I was getting confused now she was saying numbers ... was it four boys and ten girls, fourteen in total or the other way around? I could see more than five boys so that couldn't be right. Must have been the opposite, ten boys, four girls, fourteen in total.

Arrgh! Three minutes had passed and I'd forgotten to count up again! I began counting while the 'number three's' were making their way across the pool. Thirteen? What? If we were going to lose one every three minutes, there'd be none left by the time we got back to school. I counted again now they were all at the other side of the pool. Fourteen. Phew. She was right, the stand back observer role was not easy and it was rather stressful.

They continued this exercise a few times and I counted them dutifully every two minutes. The teacher was not impressed with the efforts of most of the children except for Celeste, and so she had her demonstrate the exercise to the whole class. As the swimming instructor was explaining what Celeste was doing, while she was doing it, most of the children watched carefully, hoping they'd be able to capture the essence of this wonderful aquatic being. Ford, however, was doing everything but listen ... this included; bouncing around in the water, bashing into other children, holding his breath under the water and attempting mushroom floats. The instructor barged over to me.

'Who's that boy messing in the water?!' she demanded.

'Ah, that would be Ford.'

'Ford!' she bellowed. 'Pay attention and watch this girl here.'

'That's Celeste.' She ignored that helpful comment.

'And what about that one over there?' She pointed to a dark haired child. Now was it Clio or Caprice? I couldn't tell.

'Er ...'

'Is there anything you do know?'

'This is actually the first time I've met this class. I have learnt their names, but it's quite difficult when they've got their hair wet. I think it's Clio or Caprice.'

'Is this school some kind of car dealership?'

I smirked. 'It appears so. Just shout both names, see which one answers.'

'Clio. Caprice.' Caprice turned around. I squinted and I could see the resemblance. 'Are you watching?' Caprice turned to face Celeste. 'Look at how beautifully she pushes off from the side and puts her arms together in front of her to make her body narrow so it will glide through the water more easily. When we make our bodies wide then we slow down or stop.'

Ten boys, four girls, fourteen in total.

Clio hand her hand up. 'Does that mean fat people can't glide in the water? Their bodies are wide.'

'I'm talking about the use of your arms,' the swimming instructor replied cautiously. 'Long arms to help you glide through the water.' Her words fell on deaf ears. The children practised a few more times.

Next, it was swimming around the small pool without stopping or touching the sides. Ten boys, four girls, fourteen in total. Most of the children were doing fine, despite looking like they were floundering, they were managing to tread water when the person in front slowed right down. Ford, however, was being a pain again. He was floating on his back, not doing as he should do, holding up the queue and the drifting into swimmers behind him.

'Ford! That's enough! You've been told time and time again. Get out of the pool and sit over there.' Ford began swimming away from her, right into the middle of the pool. 'Ford, I mean it, get out of the pool now.' He ignored her and carried on bouncing up and down in the centre of the pool. That's when the responsibility fell on me. 'You'll have to get him out of the pool, he needs to learn to follow my instructions.' She was assuming that he knew how to follow mine.

I climbed out of the observer's chair and crouched by the side of the pool. The other children were now finding it hard to focus on the exercise.

'Ford,' I whispered. 'Come on now.' My manipulation techniques were coming into play again coupled with bouncy voice. 'I know that you know how to make the right choice. The consequences will be much better for you if you get out now. This morning I was really impressed with your behaviour. I thought you were one of the best ones in the class.' All lies! 'I was thinking that perhaps you would have been one of the children who would win a prize.'

'Well there's no point now, I won't win it anyway.'

Now he was trying reverse psychology on me. As much as I wanted to agree with him to prove his technique wasn't working, I played along and told him what he wanted to hear.

'You never know, Ford. It all depends on your behaviour for the rest of the day, it's still possible.' It definitely wasn't, but he didn't need to know that. He thrust himself into a star float, ears under the water. I glanced over to the swimming instructor worriedly.

'These children are in your care, you need to get him out.' What did she want me to do? Climb in, swim over to him and drag him out by his hair? Knowing the ball was in his court, he began edging further away from me, to the other side of the pool. I began lumbering around the edge to get closer to him. As I neared him, he set off in a different direction, edging away again and proving that he was actually quite a good swimmer when he put his mind to it. It was just hopeless.

I tried the stern approach and played my final card, 'Ford! I've had enough now! Get out of the pool or I'll have school phone your mother.' Nothing. He didn't care.

'Right, we'll have to get the other children out then,' insisted the swimming instructor. 'Children, swim to the side and climb out please.' The rest of the group made whinging noises and then began making their way to the edge. As they were doing so, Ford climbed out of the other side and began running along the edge of the pool towards the boys changing rooms. I began power walking, my super-cool, blue shower caps scraping on the tiles, (so that was why they had so many holes) in an effort not to run on the poolside but also catch up with him. Our paths crossed just as he slipped. Luckily, (or perhaps not) I caught him.

'That's why those signs say 'no running'!' I spat, through gritted teeth. He pushed past me and fled into the changing rooms. Nine boys, four girls and one in the changing rooms, fourteen in total. Thankfully, one of the male members of staff from the swimming pool collected his things and assigned him a singular changing cubicle for him to get changed in and then stood guard outside the door until we were ready to go.

The rest of the children were given five minutes of free play until their extremely short allotted lesson time was up. They did seem to be enjoying themselves. The instructor supervised some of the children jumping in at the deep end in turn. I made the mistake of walking past them. First, the dripping wet youngsters brushed past me, despite there being ample room to get past, then I received a rather large spray when Austin attempted to do the biggest water bomb of his life yet.

Back in the changing rooms, the children readied themselves quickly and quietly. There was a lingering atmosphere among them due to what had happened. I don't think any of them could quite believe it. It was certainly not normal behaviour for children at this school. They were not allowed to put their shoes on until we got out of the changing rooms and were sitting on the bench in the foyer. I marched them through, their shoes in hand. Surprisingly, there were no shoes left behind. Even Robin had his shoes with him. Some sat on the bench, some leaned on the walls and others attempted a balancing act. If you've ever tried it, you'll know that it's rather difficult to balance one full bent leg in the air whilst standing on the other at the same time as bending over to fasten the laces in a double knot. Top marks for perseverance, Mercedes attempted this five times before giving in and sitting on the cold, tiled floor.

The children lined up when they were ready and Miss. Archer led them out to the bus. I hunted around the foyer for any traces of year three's belongings. Underneath the bench was a swimming bag. I even knew whose swimming bag it was. Trailing at the back of the line, I held the bag behind my back, out of the sight of any of the children in the class I was covering. Coming towards us was a dishevelled woman in her early twenties. Her hair was tattered and she looked exhausted. I guessed she was a newly qualified teacher, judging by the rowdy bunch pushing and shoving in a small crowd behind her. They were a rough lot. It figured. A school like that could only entice those who had no idea what they were letting themselves in for and it had happened to me once. At the back of their line, I clocked a girl with a very bad attitude, shouting rude words at our year three class. She stared at me, evil in her eyes. I wouldn't have liked to have dealt with her day in, day out.

Most of the children had climbed onto the bus with only a few of us still to get on when Robin clambered his way to the front in a panic, informing Miss Archer that he had left his bag again. I stepped onto the bus, the bag still carefully hidden.

'Mrs Harley, you haven't seen Robin's bag have you? He's left it again.' By this point, I'd nestled the bag on the front seat which Robin was stood behind, so he couldn't see it. I motioned with my eyes so Miss Archer could see that I had the bag.

'No, I'm sorry Miss Archer. I haven't seen Robin's bag,' I replied.

'Miss, I need to go and get it then.'

'No Robin, it's too late. We're not going back now, we're setting off. You should have picked it up. It's not our responsibility to look after your things. What's your mum going to say?'

'She'll kill me!' he burst out woefully and then turned on the waterworks, big time. Great, I'd made him cry ... that never looks good. My first feeling was guilt. Then I realised that it was actually justified as he obviously hadn't learnt by being told on numerous occasions and perhaps this memory would serve as a better lesson. I let him bawl it out for another three minutes before handing him the bag. I just hoped his red eyes would return to normal before we landed back at base.

Just as the bus pulled away from the curb, the fire alarm at the swimming pool started sounding. We turned the corner, which went around the back of the pool building. One of the fire doors flung open and out of it tumbled the girl I'd seen a few minutes earlier. I breathed a sigh of relief, that could have been us and I'd have had no clue what to do!

'Miss, can I sit next to you?' asked Austin.

'The bus is moving and your seat belt is on.'

'Yeah, but, I'll be really quick.'

'No Austin, that's breaking the law.'

'I do it in my car all the time at home.'

'Well you shouldn't, it's not safe.'

'It doesn't matter for a few seconds.'

'Yes, it does.'

'No it doesn't.' How had I got into one of these conversations again?

'Yes it does, that's the end of that. Talk to Roy, he's

lonely.'

Arriving at school was a welcomed break from the stress of being out and about, needing even more eyes in the back of my head. There were fifteen more minutes until lunch time and so we sat on the carpet so I could conjure up something to do.

'Okay children, the first thing we're going to do is ...' Mercedes raised her hand. 'Put your hand down Mercedes, you might find that I answer your question while I'm talking, let me finish what I have to say first.' She lowered her hand. 'So, the first thing we're going to do is ...' She raised her hand again. 'Mercedes, is it really important?' She nodded. 'Is it anything to do with what I'm talking about?' She shook her head. 'So it can't be that important ...'

'Miss, you've still got the blue shower caps on your feet!' she blurted. Everyone in the class, including me, fell about laughing. I've perfected quite a high embarrassment tolerance over the years of supply teaching. It's a good job I've learned to laugh at myself.

'Ah, thank you for that Mercedes. You've saved me from making even more of a fool of myself there. It would have been helpful if someone could have told me though before I wore them in public, outside the swimming baths, on the school bus and walking through school. But thanks anyway.'

We played *heads down, thumbs up* until the lunch bell went. It was nice to finally have some peace at long last.

ANOTHER MONDAY AFTERNOON

I was marking the pirate descriptions that the children had done earlier that day. It was always nice to have a bit of marking, something to pass the time over lunch but not loads so that I'd have to stay for hours after school.

Roy bustled in; he'd forgotten to take his lunchbox with him. He collected it from the trolley and started making his way out. I noticed a trail of liquid dripping out, all across the floor.

'Roy,' I called. 'Your lunchbox appears to be weeing.'

'Weeing?' He turned around to look behind him, spraying more liquid all over the room. 'Where?'

'Your lunch box, Roy! Put it on the table and open it.'

He did. 'Oh no! It's ruined!'

'What's ruined?'

'My lunch. It's all wet. And my ice pop's all floppy.'

'Your ice pop?'

'Yes, I bought an ice pop on the way to school, I had

a bit of it and I saved the rest to have at lunchtime.'

It was so hard to keep the giggles in. 'Well what's happened to it?'

'It's gone floppy!'

'Well yes, it's melted hasn't it?' As it so happened, I was now teaching experiential science in my lunch time. 'What would have stopped it from melting?'

'Erm ... well I didn't think it would melt.'

'A freezer. You need to keep frozen things in a freezer to stop them from melting. Go and take your lunchbox to the dinner lady, explain what has happened and ask her if you can have a school lunch.'

He skulked off, his lunchbox trailing behind, still weeing.

About twenty minutes later, when I'd almost finished marking, two children from year five or six appeared in the doorway. I saw them out of the corner of my eye. I assumed they'd be on some kind of 'duty' and left them to get on with it. For some reason, they seemed to be afraid to enter the room while I was there. I heard them muttering to each other.

'Is that year three's supply teacher?'

'I don't know. What's her name?'

'I don't know she's a supply teacher.'

'Girls, instead of asking me my name and just getting on with your usual jobs, why don't you just call me 'Mrs Supply Teacher' to save you or any of the adults (as they also have trouble remembering my real name) confusion.' They each gave me a puzzled look. Sarcasm was so much better when they actually understood. I missed secondary for that. Occasionally, a great laugh could be had with a maturing year six class. Anyhow, they scuttled in, put the afternoon's register on the desk and scuttled back out again. Why it was a two person job, I guess I'll never know.

The bell informed me that it was time to bring them inside again. I prepared myself for the cold outdoors with scarf, hat, coat and gloves. However, on my way down the corridor I was met by my class trailing in, sent in by the dinner ladies. I spun on my heel and toddled back down the corridor whilst de-garbing.

The children sat sensibly on the carpet while I took the register. As I was doing so, Miss Archer returned from lunch, coffee cup in hand. Yes, coffee *cup*, not travel mug. I too was confused. In most schools it's *illegal* to have an open hot drink. The children here must have been very trusted indeed. She popped it on the side, next to the sink. Robin had his hand up.

'Miss, how long until home time?'

'Robin, you've just come back from lunch! Stop asking how long until whenever.'

'But I didn't ask how long until whenever, I asked how long until home time.'

I ignored him.

'Miss,' Celeste whined.

'Have you got your hand up, Celeste?'

She put her hand up then whined again, 'Miss! Johnny was really mean to me at playtime. He kept on calling me Celeste.'

'Okay,' I answered, puzzled.' 'That's your name isn't it?'

'Yes, but he kept saying it!'

'Did you try walking away from him and ignoring it?' She shrugged her shoulders. 'Well if happens again, you should try doing that. Telling me in front of the whole class is giving him the attention he wants.'

'Miss!' This time it was Clio.

I raised my right arm in the air and pointed to it. 'This is what I like, hands in the air.'

She raised her arm and continued, 'Miss!'

'Yes Clio.'

'Johnny kept saying my name as well.'

'Right. What was the advice I gave Celeste?'

'Ignore him?'

'Correct. So will it be any different for you?' She shrugged her shoulders. 'No, it won't will it, so follow the same advice.' I let out a huge sigh and slumped down on the bucket chair at the front of the class.

We hadn't been left any work for the afternoon so I decided to pull out my favourite activity from the stock of afternoon art lessons I now had under my belt. The beauty about doing an art lesson is that you can usually make it work for any age and if you do it right, it can take all afternoon.

'Okay children, we're going to do an art lesson this afternoon and it's also going to be a competition.' *Competition* is a key element in making the art lesson last all afternoon. 'I'll be choosing the best picture just before we go home and that person may also choose a prize from my box. So that's three children, one each for the two best behaved children and one for the best picture.' Some of the other children who hadn't behaved particularly well now focused their attention more fervently. Ford's ears also pricked up. It was a redeeming second chance. 'The first thing you will need to do is choose a letter. I'm going to choose 'R' because I like the letter but you can choose whichever letter you like, it could be the first letter of your name.'

'But Miss, you haven't used the first letter of your

name,' stated Austin.

'I know I haven't. Harley begins with 'H'.'

'No, I mean your real name.'

'Harley is my real name.'

'He means your first name, Miss,' offered Mercedes.

'Yes. What's your first name Mrs Harley?' asked Johnny.

'It's Mrs. My first name is Mrs.'

'Eh? It can't be,' Johnny insisted.

'Yes, to be a teacher, your mum and dad have to call you Miss, Mrs or Mr at birth.' I could see the cogs whirring around in each of their little minds. I gave them a few seconds to compute their response.

'How come it says 'C. Harley' on your badge then?' questioned Mercedes. She was cleverer than I'd anticipated.

'That means your name begins with 'C',' said Johnny, triumphantly.

I chuckled at Johnny's remark. It was Mercedes had done all the brain work.

'Is it Caroline?' asked Clio. Then came the barrage.

'Is it Casey?'

'Caprice?' I grinned.

'It's Caprice isn't it? Look, she's smiling!'

'No! She's too old to be called Caprice.'

'Colin?'

'Colin's a boy's name!'

'Karen?'

'No, that's a kicking 'c' silly!'

'It might not be.'

'Right, that's enough. I wouldn't tell you if you guessed it anyway,' I moaned.

'We must have guessed it, that's why she changed

the subject. It must be Karen.'

'Okay, so you choose a letter and you draw it in the middle of your page.' I demonstrated this on the board. 'You need to make sure you draw it lightly so that you can rub it out afterwards. If you press on too hard you will be left with a ruined piece of paper and I won't be giving any more out. Next, you need to draw a line all around your letter, the same distance away all the way around. Now I can rub the middle out and I've got a letter in bubble writing that's nice and big.'

'Our teacher doesn't let us do bubble writing,' protested Mercedes. She was loyal.

'Well you best make the most of it while I'm here then. Now I've got my letter, I'm going to draw things that begin with my letter, so I'll be drawing things that begin with 'R'. I need to make sure that I'm not just drawing things around the letter, everything I draw has to be connected to the letter for a reason. Let me give you an example. Tell me some objects that begin with 'R'.'

'Rollercoaster,' offered Robin.

'Brilliant. Now, I'm going to draw my rollercoaster up the right leg of my letter and down the left leg.' I showed them and they gasped in awe. It was good, but it wasn't that good. 'Right, some more objects beginning with 'R' please.'

'Armour,' said Sienna.

'Armour begins with 'A', Sienna.'

'Ready,' offered Rocky.

'Is ready an object? It would be rather hard to draw ready wouldn't it?' I'd given in, it was easier to give them the answers myself. 'Rug is a good word. It begins with 'R' and it's easy to draw. I'm going to draw the rug underneath the letter so that it is sitting on it. When you're drawing your pictures, remember that I'm looking for a winner who tries really hard to make everything in their big picture work together. I don't want any pictures randomly drawn in the air. A bird or a plane or rain could be drawn in the air because that would make sense but not a giraffe.' Interestingly, this, they found hilarious. 'Now, is there anyone who doesn't understand what they have to do?' There were no hands.

I sent them to their tables, row by row, and began handing out the A3 paper (this is the second key element in the making activity last all afternoon). They were all eager to make a start on their winning masterpiece.

'Don't forget to draw very lightly so that you can rub it out,' I reminded them. They certainly needed reiteration.

Robin had his hand up. 'Miss, how long is it until home time?'

'There are four hours until home time.' There was actually only one hour and forty-five minutes until home time, but I get my thrills where I can.

'Four hours! That's a *really* long time.'

'Yes it is a long time. You'll have to work really hard so that it goes by quickly.' Surprisingly, none of the brighter ones picked up on it – maybe they were fed up of him too.

'Miss, can I sharpen my pencil?' whined Clio.

'Yes you may,' I replied.

'Miss, can I?' moaned Harley.

'Yes, okay,' I answered.

'Miss, me too,' said Robin.

'Yes, I suppose so,' was my response. The next thing I knew, children started getting out their seats and queuing up by the bin. 'Hang about ... what's going on here then?' It turned out that everyone needed their pencils sharpening. 'Why have we got a massive queue? Go and use another sharpener and stand at the bin over there.'

'Miss, we've only got one sharpener.' Brilliant.

'Miss Archer, is there really only one pencil sharpener in this classroom?'

'I'm afraid so.' I set her to work walking around the classroom with the bin, sharpening the pencils for all the children so that they could sit in their seats. I wanted it to look orderly in case anyone important decided to pop in; these inevitabilities should always be factored in.

Roy had begun drawing his letter already, it was an 'X'. 'Roy, what objects begin with X?'

'Xylophone?'

'Yes. What else?'

'X-ray.'

'Any more?'

'Er ...'

'Go and check in the junior dictionary.' He wandered off in search of a dictionary. Eventually he came back with a thesaurus. 'Roy, this is a thesaurus, that's why it says on the front, 'Thesaurus'. Go and find one that says 'Dictionary',' and off he toddled again.

I spun around to make my way round the classroom in the other direction, you know, for a change of scenery. Mercedes was drawing an 'A', sensible girl. Clio was drawing a 'C' and Celeste was drawing an 'S'. Ford, however, was drawing a 'V'.

'Just out of interest, Ford, how many words have you thought of beginning with V?'

'I haven't thought of any yet.'

'So how do you know you'll be able to think of enough things to make your picture really good?'

'I know what I'm going to do. I'm going to make the letter into two fingers.'

'But fingers begin with an 'F' not 'V'.'

'Yeah, but it's like, when you stick 'V's' up at someone.'

'Well as that's swearing, you won't be doing that. Choose another letter.'

'Aww ... Miss! I need another piece of paper then!'

'No you don't. If you'd have followed the instructions then you'd have drawn it ...'

'Miss, I've got a dictionary,' interjected Roy.

'Roy! Do I look like I'm in the middle of a conversation with someone?'

'Er ... no?' he replied.

'Wrong answer, I am. When two people are talking you need to stop and wait.'

'But you wanted me to get a dictionary,' he answered in confusion.

'Yes, and I still want us to look at it, but right now, Ford and I are having a conversation and you need to wait. Just because we started a conversation a few minutes ago, it hasn't carried on while I've been talking to other people.' I returned my attention to Ford. 'Sorry Ford, before we were rudely interrupted I was saying ... what was I saying?' This happened a lot. The slightest interruption and I could totally fall off the track, especially if there were a few different ones in a row. 'Oh yes, I remember. If you had followed the instructions in the first place then you would be able to rub out what you had drawn because you would have been drawing lightly.'

'But I can't,' he whined. 'I've pressed on too hard.'

'That's a problem you'll have to deal with.' I'd end up regretting using those words later on.

'Please Miss, just this once.'

'If I let you have another piece of paper, then I have to make thirty more pieces of paper available for the other children to use to make it fair. The answer is no, turn the paper over.' He snatched the paper and turned it over in a strop, causing it to crease slightly.

To be fair, Roy had waited patiently since we had had words and so we set about looking in the dictionary. He handed it to me.

'Why are you giving it to me, Roy?'

He shrugged.

'Have you had a look yourself?'

He gave me the blank stare I'd become accustomed to when asking certain children to do a bit of dictionary work.

'What should you be looking for Roy?'

'Xylophone?'

'Sort of, we're actually looking for the letter 'X' to start with aren't we? How do we find it?'

'Flick the pages?'

'We can do that. Are we looking for 'X' on a random page or will it be in a certain place, following on from another letter?'

'Random?' It always baffles me when children choose the wrong answer when I've given them a choice. Especially as it's usually obvious and it would be really hard to think up the real answer as the untrue yet detailed alternative.

'Could it be possible that the letters the words begin with are in alphabetical order?'

'Er ... no, I don't think so.'

'I see. So how will they be arranged then?'

'The words are just in the book.'

'Well I think that the dictionary is cleverer than you thought. I think that it wants to help people find words in it and so all the words are in alphabetical order. Do you know what that is?'

He screwed his face up.

'It means that they are in the same order as the alphabet. What letter comes before 'X'?' I could see him singing the alphabet to himself in his head.

'W?' Thank goodness he knew the alphabet.

'Excellent! Now 'W' and 'X' are near the end of the alphabet so let's flick through to the back of the book.' We'd found it, 'X'. 'What words does it say under 'X'?'

'Xylophone and X-ray.'

'Correct. Are there any more?'

'No.'

'Can you make a really good picture with only two ideas?'

'No.'

'You best choose another letter then.' He looked at me with pursed lips and puppy dog eyes, disappointment written all over his face. 'Why don't you try 'R' for Roy? I've already given you some good ideas.'

At the other side of the classroom, Rocky was still struggling with drawing his letter. He'd drawn it lightly every time but he was making a mess of it.

'Rocky, why is your letter so small?'

'I can't do it, Miss, can you draw it for me?'

'If I draw it for you it won't be your work and you also won't be able to win the prize because it's a competition.'

'Oh yeah.'

'Follow the steps I told you.' I showed him again on a white board before meandering around the classroom again. I've considered purchasing a pedometer to record how many miles I walk around classrooms every day. It really is the best way to look like you're busy when the head teacher pops their head around the door though, especially as I never usually know who any of the adults are. I've met plenty of head teachers without realising. I think they assume that supply teachers must go scouring the school websites looking at pictures of all the head teachers in the area. Sometimes they've got his, 'Don't you know who I am?' kind of thing going on.

Jensen was hard at work on his picture. He was quite good at drawing and had included lots of detail on his elephant.

'That's a beautiful elephant, Jensen, you're very good at drawing. I've just got two questions for you though. The first one … why is your elephant in the air?'

'It's Dumbo.'

'Ah, ok, I can understand that. So it would make sense then, wouldn't it, if your letter was 'E' or even 'D'. Why is your letter 'L'?'

'It's 'L' for elephant.' Of course it was. 'L' for L-i-fant. As wrong as it is, I didn't have the heart to tell him, I just minced backwards, away from him. Unfortunately, it was likely that someone would notice and tell him later on.

As I stepped backwards I tripped over Dino, who was skulking around the classroom.

'Dino, why are you out of your seat?' I asked.

'Miss, I was just asking if I could borrow a rubber,' he answered.

'No he wasn't, Miss, he just came over to chat to

Austin,' snitched Clio.

'No I didn't!' he proclaimed, 'Miss! She's lying!' I really couldn't be bothered.

'Dino, did you come to borrow a rubber?'

'Yes.'

'So, if I trust you to borrow my rubber, you can return to your seat and there will be no more problems will there?' He shook his head. I routed through my pencil case and then handed him the rubber. 'Please be very careful with it. I don't lend my rubber out to just anyone. I don't want it damaged, it's an expensive rubber.' And it was, it was for my own use so I'd bought a decent one that did the job well, unlike the usual school resources.

I toddled over to see how Ford was getting on. He was working tirelessly. There was something not quite right.

'Ford, that doesn't look like the piece of paper that you had before. Have you got a new piece of paper?' His chest sunk in and his head and shoulders bent over it. He stared up at me, the whites of his eyes showing below his pupils with his lips held tightly together. Now that was guilt if I ever saw it! 'Ford, I'm speaking to you. Have you got a new piece of paper?'

'Yes.'

'Who told you that you could get a clean piece of paper?' Now at this point, I was expecting him to tell me that he'd told Miss Archer a sob story and she'd let him get a new piece of paper. 'Well?' He shook his head at me. 'Are you trying to tell me that nobody has said you can get a clean piece of paper?' He nodded. 'So you've just gone ahead anyway and helped yourself because you knew I'd say no?' He nodded again. 'Right, that's it!

I've had enough of you. You've had a terrible day making all the wrong choices. Go and sit on the carpet.' He kicked his chair back to annoy me even more (and it worked) then stomped over to the carpet area and threw himself down. It was twenty to two. 'You need to stay on the carpet for five minutes. When it gets to quarter to two then you can go back to your seat.'

'But Miss, I can't tell the time.'

'Can you see that the big hand is on eight now?'

'Yeah,' he said sulkily.

'How long until home time, Miss?' shouted Robin.

'Not now Robin! I'm in the middle of a conversation and you're interrupting me. When the big hand gets to nine then you can go back to your table.'

'Okay.'

Just as I turned around Robin was there, out of his seat, again!

'Robin! For goodness sake, sit down! It's an hour and twenty minutes until home time so stop asking me!'

'Only an hour and twenty minutes? Wow! That's gone fast.' Darn it! In the stressfulness of it all I'd given the game away and revealed the *actual* length of time until home time. I was losing my small pleasures, and fast.

Quite a few of the children were getting to the point where they had filled their pages with lots of little drawings.

'Miss, can I colour it now?' asked Mercedes. It was time to move onto the next element of the 'making it last all afternoon' plan.

'Before colouring, we can make our artwork look really professional by getting a black fine line felt tip or a black handwriting pen and drawing over all over pencil marks carefully. Then we let it dry and rub the pencil marks out afterwards.'

'What? All of it?'

'Yes, all of it. Every last stroke of the pencil.'

'That'll take me ages!'

'Precisely.'

'Pardon?' It wasn't a rude 'pardon' she just didn't understand what I'd said, thankfully.

'But it will look excellent in the end!'

She looked at me as if to say 'will it?' and then marched back to her seat, black fine liner in hand.

Over the next ten minutes I handed out many black fine liner felt tips in attempt to drag the activity out to last all afternoon. I was over at the table near the carpet area and noticed that Ford was still sat on the carpet. It was now 1:55pm.

'Ford, what are you still doing on the carpet?' I asked curiously.

'I did as you said, I sat on the carpet,' he replied grumpily.

'I said that you could go back to your table when the big hand got to nine.'

'I know, but I wasn't looking at the clock then and now it's on ten so I don't know what to do!' he whined. I suppressed a grin and chuckled on the inside. Knowing I was laughing at him would really not have been helpful in this situation.

'I see. Well as the big hand is past nine you may go and continue with your work. Luckily for you, I'm not expecting you to sit there for another fifty-five minutes until the big hand reaches nine again.' He crawled halfway across the carpet until he caught me giving him 'the look' and then he walked sensibly back to his seat.

'Miss, I've finished,' boasted Mercedes. Finished!?!? The alarm bells started ringing ... it was impossible. There was an hour left! When I'd walked over I realised that she meant that she'd finished outlining her picture and rubbing out the pencil marks. Still, an hour was a very long time to colour it in. I searched for a more time consuming alternative and found it ... watercolour pencils! After all, the aim was that they'd never actually finish the activity because then what would they do?

'Now colour your picture carefully with these watercolour pencils. When you've done a few sections, you can start brushing over it lightly with a small amount of water to create different effects.' I showed her an example and off she went. I stopped the rest of the class to brief and instruct them on the pending variation of activity.

Just as there was a flurry of activity and there were at least ten children out of their seats, collecting things they needed for the transition in activity, an adult paid us a visit. Brilliant! It was just typical. To my surprise, she'd brought with her a fresh cup of coffee for Miss Archer (in a normal coffee cup again) and it looked like she was doing the rounds for all the regular staff. Miss Archer thanked her profusely as she obviously thought she needed it this afternoon. She popped it on the draining board along with the other cup.

It was at that moment I realised that I hadn't seen my rubber in over twenty minutes.

'Dino, could I have my rubber back now please?'

'I haven't got it,' he replied.

'Haven't got it? How is that even possible? I trusted you with my rubber and I told you I don't lend it out to anyone so where is it?'

'Rocky wanted to borrow it so I gave it to him.'

'You lent my rubber to someone else without asking?'

'Umm … yes.' I could feel the anger rising up inside of me.

'Rocky, where's my rubber?'

'I don't have it,' he said, shirking all responsibility.

'So where is it then?'

'I gave it to Roy.'

'Roy?' I spat, turning to him. He gave me a very sheepish look and slid down into his seat.

Celeste grassed him up, 'Miss, I saw him chuck it over there onto the side.' Sure enough, my rubber was on the side. It had previously still been in its cardboard holder to keep the majority of it clean. It now had a half a ripped cover around it. On one side were two big, googly eyes, drawn very badly with handwriting pen and on the other side was a mouth with a tongue sticking out. Why was I stupid enough to trust kids with stuff?!

'Was this your doing, Roy?'

'No Miss, it wasn't me,' he insisted.

'Was it like this when you had it, Rocky?' He shook his head. 'Did you see Roy draw this Celeste?' She nodded her head. 'Go and sit on the carpet for fifteen minutes, Roy. I'm taking away ten minutes of your golden time too.'

By now there were quite a few people on to brushing their pictures with water. Miss Archer was assisting Clio over by the sink. She took a sip of her hot coffee while she warmed her hands around the cup and then returned it to the draining board. I had the feeling that it must have been school policy to keep the drinks on the draining board in case they got knocked over.

That would be why she was hovering around the sink. I looked at her, wishing I'd been given the opportunity to have such a comfort at a time like this. Her hand was still around the mug, extracting all the warmth it could give.

A while later, Roy had begun his watercolours and strode over to the sink to collect a paintbrush and some water. Being Roy, he didn't think to get a clean pot and fill it with clean water. Instead, he inspected all the dirty pots filled with dirty paint water on the draining board. Before returning to his seat he thought he'd have a little play with the water. He dipped his paintbrush into the first dirty water pot and gave it a swirl, then the second, then the third. After a while, he realised he was quite enjoying himself mixing all the colours up and he included the cold pot of coffee, after all, no-one was drinking it so it would be okay. That's when he slipped up. Miss Archer took her hand away from her coffee cup for a moment to help Dino with his shoelaces and ... splash, in went the paintbrush! Murky green ribbons formed and danced in the liquid. In a panic he stirred it up quickly as there wasn't a lot, hoping the colour would disappear and it did to some extent. Miss Archer reached for her coffee cup and brought it to her lips. I tried to rescue her.

'Miss Archer ...' Unfortunately, she decided to take a drink of coffee before turning my way. She hadn't noticed. Roy looked at me, dread all over his face, expecting a terrible punishment. I brought my fingers to my lips as I stared him down, it would be our little secret. After all, I'd watched him in amazement for the past five minutes and a little paint never hurt anyone ... well, hopefully not, but I guess I'll never know.

I started doing the rounds again. There were some

brilliant pieces of work. Caprice was still on the pencil drawing stage. I know that I wanted the activity to drag out all afternoon, but there were only twenty minutes until home time.

'Caprice, your picture is really good, but I'd have expected to see you on the watercolour stage by now.'

'I just want it to be perfect, Miss. I'm stuck now though because I don't know how to draw Australia.'

'Why would you need to draw Australia? You've chosen the letter 'O'.' She'd drawn some great things, an octopus, olives, an oven and even an otter.

'Yeah, 'O' for Australia.'

'I've got some good news for you then ... Australia begins with an 'A'!'

It was time to pack away and so I requested the attention of the whole class. There was a lot to do in fifteen minutes. I began giving out the instructions and of course they all started muttering and fidgeting after the first one, not bothering to listen to any of the others. I stopped again and waited for them to finish wittering. To ensure a quick tidy up I gave out the jobs to the sensible kids so that I could crowd control the rest and ask them to do anything and everything to keep them looking and feeling busy like; 'neaten up that pile of papers, pick up five tiny pieces of paper off the floor, group the pencil crayons in colours', anything to keep them doing something that didn't involve running around stupidly and 'play' fighting with someone else.

Once they had done their jobs they sat quietly on the carpet. I was surprised at how quickly they had managed to bottom the room and they hadn't done a bad job either, obviously, it was down to my excellent organisational skills.

'How long until home time, Miss?' I didn't even have to look at who had said that, I already knew.

'Home time is in five minutes, Robin,' I sighed in relief.

'Yes!' he hissed as he pulled his clenched fist towards himself. He lived for playtime, lunch time and home time. It doesn't change for some as they get older really does it, many adults live for the weekend.

The bucket chair at the front of the carpet area had been piled up with the children's work as I had previously instructed, so I chose to sit on an ordinary chair that was like the rest in the class that was already conveniently positioned next to it. Just as I was bending to sit, I noticed a piece of paper under it that had been missed.

'Roy, can you put that piece of paper in...' CRASH! BANG! WALLOP! I'd bounced onto the chair and then landed firmly on my bottom, the chair leaning on my shoulder. The children must have found it shocking because they didn't laugh, instead they gasped. I'd have laughed! I fished under my bottom for the piece of paper to give to Roy. It read 'Broken chair – DO NOT USE'. My shoulders began heaving up and down rhythmically.

'Miss, are you alright?'

'No she's not, she's crying!'

'She isn't! She's laughing.'

'Miss, are you crying?' I voiced my laughter to put them out of their misery and they laughed along with me. Roy helped me up and I hobbled over to the door.

'Okay year three, boys first, collect your belongings and line up, then the girls.' I walked them to the exit door where the parents were waiting for them. I bounced the door while the children came up to me one by one and pointed to who they were going home with. When there were about three children left, Johnny's mum approached me. I'd sent Johnny out five minutes previously.

'I just wanted to check, we've been looking for Johnny's homework in his book bag for five minutes and we can't find it. Now he tells me that he didn't get any, but I know he must be lying because this morning you told me that you'd make sure Johnny got some homework tonight so he's lost it in the classroom somewhere.'

'No, I didn't actually say that. I said I'd do my best. We've had a very hectic day and none of the children have got homework. I'm sure the teacher will sort it out tomorrow when she gets back.'

'But I want him to do homework tonight.'

'I'm afraid there is no homework tonight. You know, it's not actually an obligation for primary schools to set homework.'

'Well that's ridiculous! How am I supposed to do home learning with him?'

'Well you could always make it up or buy a workbook at any good bookshop or supermarket for that matter.' She stormed off in a huff and I was glad. I was sure I was going be complained about the following day. The remaining three turned into the remaining one and it was now fifteen minutes since the bell had gone. It was just Caprice and me. Miss Archer told me that I needed to take her to the office.

'Miss,' she whined on the way. 'Who's going to get that prize?' I couldn't believe I'd forgotten! Poor kids. Caprice was a rather sly dog though, waiting until all the children had gone and the only option was her.

'Oh no! I forgot, didn't I?'

'I'm the only one left,' she replied gleefully.

'Don't worry, when you've gone, I'll choose some people and leave some prizes for them and a note for Miss Archer.'

Her face dropped.

Upon arrival at the office we were met by two other teachers and two other children. I was expecting to drop Caprice off and have done with it, but no. Each teacher was required to wait with their child, even though that meant all of us wasting a further ten minutes just standing there. Caprice was the last one to be picked up, and no, her parent did not apologise for being twenty-five minutes late. As far as he was concerned, it was all part of the free government childcare service I was involved with providing. I was just thankful that I'd done all the marking at lunchtime.

I staggered back to the classroom. Just as I approached the door the year four teacher stopped me.

'I just came to let you know it's the staff meeting in five minutes,' she said. Why on earth was she telling me that?

'Oh, okay, and is it in my classroom then?' That was the only possible reason I could think of for her purposefully coming to inform me.

'No, it's in year six as usual.'

'Right ... and what time does it go on until?'

'Five o'clock.' Five o'clock! I'd have been home for nearly an hour by then!

'Why exactly are you telling me this?'

'ALL staff need to go to the staff meeting. I'm telling you so you can come.'

It's naughty, but I laughed in her face. For the

first time, I was ecstatic that my badge had VISITOR in red letters plastered all over it. 'And what would be the benefit in me coming along, especially now I've finished my days work at this school?' I received no response, she just turned round and headed towards year six, so as not be late for the staff meeting.

When I could no longer see her I returned to year three's classroom. The cleaner was in there, cleaning.

'Oh hello, love, I've not seen you before, are you new?'

'No I've just been here for the day.'

'Ah, are you a supply teacher?' Yes, it's my job *and* my name.

'I am.'

'Ooh, it's a tough job that one.' Is it? Have you done it?

'Oh it's not so bad,' I blathered.

'Is that what you want to be then? A teacher?'

'I am a teacher.'

'No, I mean when you've finished your training.' What kind of supply teachers had she seen before? They must have all been really young!

'I have finished my training.'

'But I mean when you're older, do you want to have a class like this when you're grown up?' Now okay, I'm twenty-eight which isn't really old, but it's not young either. And yes, I'm often mistaken for being considerably younger than that with my ever so youthful looks that are quickly fading away in this job, but seriously, 'when you grow up?'

'I am a grown-up. I'm in my seventh year of teaching?'

'Really? You don't look old enough!' she remarked.

'Did you not fancy getting a real job then?' I wasn't aware until now that supply teaching is a pretend job.

'Nah, pretend job all the way for me. Anyway, I need to be going now. See you again sometime.' I sauntered out of the classroom, gleefully passing the year six classroom where the door was ajar. I peered in and grinned at the year four teacher staring at me cruelly as I passed. Oh, how good it was to have a 'pretend job'!

A TIME WASTER DAY

It was 7:10am and I really didn't want to get out of bed. I was already running a bit late for a morning call. I dragged myself out anyhow. There was so much to be done that day if I didn't get a call, like, writing a book! 7:15am, the phone rang.

'Hi Carly, I've got a booking for you today at Spenable School in year six.'

'Spenable? Where is it? I've never heard of it.'

'It's thirty miles away from you, right in the countryside, it's a lovely location.'

'Have you not got any teachers a bit nearer?'

'Well it's a new contract and you've had lots of good feedback.'

'That's really nice and everything, but I'm not travelling thirty miles.'

'I just thought that it'd be easy for you to get to as it's straight on the motorway.' Who would have thought that you'd need to be good at geography to be a supply teaching agent? My house is nowhere near the motorway and as far as I'm aware, going on the motorway slows you down even more.

'I think I'll pass on that one.'

'Okay, well thanks anyway, we'll give you a call if anything else comes in.'

Back to attempting to drag myself out of bed. Much buzzing again. I was never going to get in the shower at this rate. Another agency.

'Hi Carly, I've got work for you today in year four.'

'Brilliant, where is it?'

'Only three miles away from you. Are you available?' Of course I was available, would I ask about the school if I wasn't?

'Yes, I'm available.'

'Okay, I'll e-mail the details through for you.' That was the incentive I needed to get a shift on.

Whilst getting ready I received yet another call from another agency.

'Hi Carly, are you available today?'

'Sorry I've just been booked.'

'Oh that's a shame, it's a really nice school and they've asked for you. Never mind, I'll tell them you're busy.'

I was ready for leaving the house forty minutes later and began scraping the frost off my car. That's when my phone rang again. It was the second agency.

'Really sorry about this, Carly, but the school have made a mistake, they don't need you anymore. You haven't set off have you?'

'No, but I was about to.'

'Like I said, I'm really sorry. It's not like the school to mess us about, they were really apologetic. I promise I'll give you the first thing that comes in next.' I rung off. I was annoyed but it wasn't her fault. I decided to give the third agency a call about the work I'd turned down.

'Hi, it's Carly Harley. It turns out I'm available now as the school have just cancelled so I wondered if that day close by was still available?'

'Oh, I'm sorry Carly, I've given that away now.' It was to be expected.

I busied myself in the house for over two hours when the agency who had promised to give me the first booking they had in, called. It was now 9:58am.

'Hi Carly, I've got a booking for you this afternoon as a cover supervisor in a secondary school.'

'Secondary? A cover supervisor?'

'Yes, I thought you used to do secondary.'

'I did. There's a reason I do primary now. Besides, as a cover supervisor, you expect me to do the same job for half the pay.'

'Well no, it's just supervising. The children will know what they're doing.'

'No they won't, it'll be the same job and I'll end up doing it anyway.'

'Yes, I see your point.' (That was definitely an admission.) 'If we get anything else in, you'll be the first one we'll call.' I didn't hold my breath and it's a good job because I'd have been dead.

THURSDAY MORNING

I'd been booked on the previous day and so organisation and punctuality were on my side. I pulled up at the school gates before the barrier, wound my window down and reached for the buzzer. Too far away. I don't know what it is about those buttons but I can never get my car close enough. I'm always afraid of knocking my wing mirror off or something. I slipped out of my car in order to press the button. By this point, there was already a car behind me, waiting to get in.

I pressed the button and waited. No response. I couldn't even hear the usual crackling, informing me that they were attempting to respond. I pressed again. Nothing. I had this vision of the office staff in the staffroom together, making themselves cups of tea and raiding the milk for their bowls of cereal that they'd later blame on the supply teachers. Perhaps they were in there waiting for the *teacher's* briefing. I waited a little longer before pressing again. There were now five cars behind me and they'd started beeping their horns. If another car was to join our queue it would be out on the main road, blocking all the traffic.

It was not the first car behind me or the second car or even the third that attempted to assist me. It was in fact the fifth car. In my wing mirror I could see him abandon his vehicle and begin walking up the street towards me. The situation was so embarrassing, but hopefully he'd be able to get me out of it. As he approached he waved his fob at the meter and like magic it began lifting upwards and I drove in.

After parking up in a space near the exit, to avoid being blocked in by an over enthusiastic member of staff staying at school until after four, I followed the signs to reception and was 'greeted' by the lady on the desk.

'Who are you?'

'Carly Harley, supply.'

'Oh, how did you get in? We have to let supply teachers in from here. Don't you have a car?'

'Yes, I have a car. I was pressing the button and it wasn't getting me anywhere. I was causing a five car hold up until someone kind came and swiped me in.'

'Right, well, they shouldn't have done that without knowing who you are.'

'I was blocking the way so he didn't really have a choice.'

'Okay, well you're here now. Carly did you say?'

'Yes, Carly.'

'Right, can I see some photo ID and your CRB please?' It was a good job I'd remembered them. I handed them over and she studied them carefully. 'Date of birth?'

'Pardon?'

'What's your date of birth?' I gave it to her and she checked it on my driving licence. This was very weird.

She took my documents and photocopied them. Technically, she's not supposed to do that but she wasn't the first, and no, she didn't ask me if it was okay. After she'd done that she pulled out a file, it looked like it was full of information from the agency about various teachers. The photo that the agency had taken the day I'd signed up was there and she compared my face, the photo and my driving licence. I wondered if she'd previously worked for passport control. 'Any previous convictions?' It said all that on my CRB didn't it?

'No.'

'Not even a driving offence?'

'No, and it does state that on my CRB.'

'I'm just checking that it actually belongs to you. Anyhow, I think that'll be okay.' With such thorough checking I'd have hoped that she'd have known for certain that it was more than 'okay'. 'Here's our information pack for supply teachers, you need to read it thoroughly and familiarise yourself with all the protocols.' It was a twenty page document. When did she suppose I'd have time to read all that? It wasn't actually for supply teachers anyway, it was the full staff handbook for new staff. The only useful bit was the times of the school day – most importantly, home time! 'Just sign in and I'll take you down.' No fancy sign-in machines, no cameras, no stickers and no badges saying VISITOR in big letters, so after the Spanish inquisition rigmarole it was a simple, just sign-in and off you go.

The first place she took me was to the head teacher's office. This was very unusual. Perhaps they actually wanted me to know who would to be watching me closely (but trying not to make it obvious) all day. Just as we arrived he was leaving his room. In one hand I was armed with my very big, heavy supply bag that houses at least six text books, a pencil case, a box of prizes, a lunchbox with lunch in, a bottle of water, a toilet roll (for snotty noses or bathroom emergencies), timesheets and anything else I can fit it in it. In the other hand I was just about managing to keep hold of the twenty page document, my CRB, driving licence and my travel cup which at that moment was filled with hot, decent coffee from home, made with hot milk of course.

'Ah good morning, I'm Mr Thorn...' Despite observing the fact that I was loaded up like a donkey, and as a man, apparently being observant comes more naturally, the head teacher still insisted on thrusting out his hand to shake mine as he introduced himself. I fumbled around and managed to balance everything in my right hand. I put out my left hand and then realised it was the wrong hand and then fumbled around again and balanced everything in the other arm and then shook his hand feebly in an attempt not to drop anything. He had a strong grip that almost caused me to lose my handle of my precious coffee. 'And you are ...' he looked over to the lady from reception to inform him of my name. This was a rare moment. Instead of putting her out of her misery and telling Mr Thorn what my name was myself, I looked at her too, in anticipation, could she remember my name? Unlikely.

'This is the supply teacher covering in year five today,' she stuttered. Classic ... supply teacher.

'And does this supply teacher have a name?' he said sarcastically, then turning his attention to me. Impressive!

'It's Mrs Harley, but don't worry, I often answer to 'supply teacher', some days I think it's my actual name.'

He didn't have a sense of humour. He didn't laugh. Strike one. He just breathed in through his nose whilst tilting his head backwards, lips tightly together turning downwards at the corners and continued his journey to wherever he was going.

The receptionist and I did not exchange any more words. When we arrived at the classroom she pointed inside and then toddled off while I set out to explore. The first thing I did, as usual, was to put my bag and coat by the desk and search for any evidence of notes left by the teacher. There was a printed letter for my perusal;

Dear Supply Teacher,

School starts at 8:50am. You will need to collect the children from the playground. Only about half of them will turn up then, go inside anyway with half and then the rest will drift into your classroom late.

9:00 – Register – Someone will bring the lunch register, the actual register is on the computer. Ask the teacher next door to sign you in on my log in.

9:10 – Numeracy – The children are doing a test. It will need marking afterwards, I've left the mark scheme out for you. The test should be done in SATs conditions, they will need a ruler, mirror, protractor, pencil and tracing paper. It is a NON- CALCULATOR test.

10:10 – Assembly in the hall.

10:30 – I have swapped my duty with another teacher so

you will need to cover it for them today.

10:45 – Literacy – They are working on a World War Two project in topic. I've booked the laptops for you but you'll need to collect them. They can research all lesson.

11:45 – Guided Reading – You will need to read with two separate groups, twenty minutes for each.

12:30 – Lunch

Thanks for today and by the way, I've told them that we're friends and you'll be reporting to me everything that they do when we go for drink tonight.

Mr Jones

Okay, so firstly, what about the afternoon? Secondly, mark all the tests?! That would come under assessment, which was definitely not my job and would take me forever! Thirdly, you've swapped your duty so the supply teacher can do it – cheers for that. Also, the only thing I could be thankful for about the laptop lesson was no marking. The stupid things are great at conking out because they haven't been plugged in and as for guided reading ... it's bad enough expecting someone else to pick up what your groups are doing, managing it all is even worse, especially when it lasts 45 minutes because it's two sessions lumped together. Guided reading works best when it is 20 minutes long. Supply teachers like INDEPENDENT READING. It's easy, controlled and best of all ... quiet. Besides informing me that we were good friends, he'd left me no more indication about his life to carry out the fictitious scenario he'd invented.

I went next door to the other year five teacher to see if she could log me on and shed some light on the afternoon. Nobody there. The next classroom on was year six and thankfully, there was a teacher in there.

'Hi, I'm covering in year five today and I was hoping to be logged on in Mr Jones's name. He's left instructions sanctioning that to happen.'

'I've no idea what his log on is. You'll have to ask someone else,' she said, snottily. To be fair, being snotty was part of her school role, being a year six teacher and all, but I wasn't going to give up just yet.

'Okay, I was also wondering about this afternoon though. I've been booked for all day but there are only instructions for this morning. Is it only a morning booking?'

'You're going to have to ask at reception. The cover supervisor usually covers that class on Thursday afternoons as it's his PPA.' I suppose she'd been sort of helpful.

I made my way back down to reception. 'Excuse me, I'm confused about where I should be this afternoon,' I said to the lady at the desk.

'Yes, we realise now that you won't be needed in year five. Come back at the end of lunch time and we'll have sorted something out for you to do.' Sounded ominous. I wanted to know how the day was going to pan out. I also knew that it would take up a chunk of lunch time that I needed for marking those blasted tests that he'd cleverly set. I hoped that appropriate work was going to be set for the afternoon if I wasn't going to find out what was happening till then, otherwise, I'd have to think it up on my feet in only a few minutes.

On the way back from my walkabout around school I stuck my head around the door of the other year five classroom again. The teacher was in.

'Hi, I'm covering in year five this morning. I've got some instructions here from Mr Jones asking me to ask you to sign me in.'

'Oh yes, of course, love, that's not a problem. I'll do it now and get you into the register as well.'

That was great, I was getting some things sorted. I followed her into my classroom and she sorted the computer out for me.

'Is there anything else you need?'

'No, I think I'm okay for now, thank you.'

'Well if there is anything, just send one of the children through and I'll do my best to help you out.'

'Thank you, that's really kind,' I said gratefully and off she went back to her classroom.

Whilst I waited for the bell to ring, I took the opportunity to eat my breakfast and put out all the resources the children needed for the test. There were three separate tests in total to cover all abilities, with a list of names for each one. When I heard the bell, I made my way out to the playground and stood in between two of the other teachers.

'Is this where Mr Jones's class lines up?' I received a nod. One by one, children came and stood in front of me. Every last one of them questioned who I was.

'Are you teaching us today?'

'Are you Mr Jones's friend?'

'Will you be seeing Mr Jones later?'

'Do you know Mr Jones's brother?' Of course I

answered 'yes' to all of those queries, hoping later on I would not trip myself or Mr Jones up. The other teachers had started taking their classes in and I only had five children. I doubted that I had half of the class but I followed suit and went in anyway. The last thing I wanted was to get locked out.

On arrival at the classroom, I was surprised to find five more children in the room, causing mischief.

'Why are you in the classroom on your own?' I asked sternly.

'We always come in after breakfast club,' responded a small boy who looked like he should be in a class a few years younger.

'Without an adult?'

'Sometimes.'

'Right then, year five, could we get out our reading books and sit in our morning places please. I'd like to hear silent reading.'

'How can you hear silence? It's silent,' the young looking kid piped up.

'You can, it's a golden sound,' I heard myself and cringed, it was like listening to my year seven English teacher, Mr Worthwell. 'Off you go,' I chuntered at him. He stood there for a few seconds more, puzzling it out and then, by the look of it, gave it no more attention and went off in search of a book. After a minute or so, I called after him, 'What's your name then?' I had a feeling it would be useful to learn his early on.

'Me?' Of course you! Who else? But instead, I nodded politely. 'Nathan.'

'Okay Nathan, why are you wandering around the classroom? Get the book from your book bag like everyone else has.'

'Oh Miss, I can't. I've forgotten my book bag.'

'How convenient. Have you got a book in your drawer that you're reading?'

'No. We just have the ones in our book bags.'

'You best choose a book from the bookshelf then, quickly!' He set to work looking for a book whilst I paraded around the classroom checking the children were reading quietly and greeting the stream of children trailing in and instructing them to get out their reading books.

One of the children came in with his parent. I watched her as she put his coat on his hook, book bag in the box and his reading book in his drawer. He just walked off to chat to his friend.

'Reading books please,' I repeated. I wanted to deal with the fact he was talking without directly addressing him while his mother was there. You can never tell how they'll react. The last thing I wanted was a showdown in front of the whole class for telling her son what to do. In some cases you'd think school rules don't apply until the parent has left the building, it's no wonder most schools don't let them in!

Before she left she stared at the board for a few moments and then meandered over to me. 'So you're a supply teacher then?'

'Yes.'

'Are you a supply teacher because you can't spell?'

'Excuse me?'

'It says 'Febuary' on the board.' I studied the word February. She was right, it was wrong, but I hadn't written it.

'You're right, it is wrong. I didn't actually write it though so I'm afraid I can't take any responsibility.' She shrugged her shoulders and left. I was slightly concerned as it was now the seventeenth of February. I changed the spelling, with my own board pen of course, and then out of curiosity, I tracked down the Literacy books and had a peek as I know lots of teachers write the month on the board once a month and change the days and dates accordingly. The whole class had been spelling 'February' wrong all month. And they say our education system is going to the dogs.

Five minutes had passed and Nathan was still looking for a book. It's hard when you don't know them because if I had have known him and what level he was on, I'd have chosen him a book in the first place and made him sit down with it.

'Nathan, you've still not chosen a book. I'm going to count from ten to one. If you haven't chosen a book by then and sat down with it, I'm going to take five minutes off your play time for the five minutes you've just wasted. Ten ... nine ... eight.' It wasn't until eight that he started moving. He obviously needed less time so I sped up. 'Seven ... six ... five.' He purposefully picked a book from the middle of the shelf, one he'd probably being eyeing up all this time for a situation such as this, but had just been stalling. 'Four ... three ...' He made his way over to the chair. 'Two ... one!' His bottom hit the chair just as I said 'one'. 'That was a close call, Nathan, you'll have to be quicker next time because I'll count quickly and from five!'

I strolled around the class trying to learn some of the children's names.

'What's your name?' I asked the plump, white-blonde haired boy.

'Ben,' he replied.

The girl sat next to him butted in, 'We've got two Ben's in this class. This one is Ben Munter and that one is Ben Drover,' she said, pointing to the 'other' Ben.

'Sorry, did you say that boy is called Ben Dover?'

'No, Ben D-R-OVER.'

'Ah I see.' She'd not noticed the fun in the alternative name, but I bet his parents had. What were they thinking? Most of the children seemed to have filtered in so I walked over to the laptop at the front to take the register. The computer had locked as I hadn't touched it in the last fifteen minutes and it needed unlocking with Mr Jones's password. Despite being an annoying chore, it was a good opportunity to put Nathan to work on an errand. All teachers know that sending a potentially naughty child on an errand at the beginning of the day is a non-verbal and secret way of saying to the child 'I trust you', although it probably isn't true. If it works you can earn their respect because apparently, you 'trust' them. I've noticed that on supply it can be doubly effective. Sometimes, the child then seems to believe that you haven't noticed that they're usually naughty and they think if they're good all day you'll be fooled. Usually I'm not, but it makes my life much easier when they try it and I'll do anything to encourage it and I love playing along pretending to be fooled.

'Nathan, I need your help.' (Bouncy voice needed.)

'Me?'

'Yes you. I need you to do me a massive favour. Just look at this computer. I can't possibly get in so I'm going to need you to go next door and ask an adult to help me. I just knew you'd be the best person for the job, I'm sure you know all the adults in the next class.'

'Yes I do! I know all of them.'

'Excellent! So you'll be really helping me out by sorting this problem out for me. Without you, I can't even do the register.'

'Okay Miss, I'll do it straight away!' he beamed enthusiastically. It had worked a treat ... changed child. He walked to the next classroom sensibly, smartly and purposefully. If only he knew I'd played him like a fiddle. Some people think that a large part of teaching is behaviour management, but I like to think of it in real terms as 'manipulation techniques'. Moments later he returned with the teacher from next door and she unlocked it for me.

'Sorry about this, Miss,' I said apologetically.

'It's alright, don't worry about it. You've just got to touch the mouse or interactive whiteboard every five minutes so it doesn't go off. The children are really good at remembering.' Sounded like an excuse to get of their seats to me.

'Okay. Can you give me the password in case it happens again?'

'Oh no, I'm afraid I can't do that. I'm the e-safety coordinator. I can't allow it.' Had she not just logged me on in someone else's name?

'Um ... okay. So if it happens again we'll just send for you again.'

'Yes that's fine, but just remember to keep touching the mouse or board.'

'Will do.' I had no intention of letting that be the bane of my life all morning. 'Thank you. Well done Nathan, what a superstar!' I exaggerated.

After the register, I went through my usual spiel in my bouncy voice as they were all now in class. 'Ooh's' and 'ah's' were heard when the prize box made an appearance and everyone raised their hand when I asked, 'Who thinks they'll win one of my prizes?' I was looking at having a good day.

'Okay children, you'll probably have noticed all the equipment on your tables and that's because we're going to be doing a Maths test.' Sighs and moans rippled all over the room. 'It will be SATs conditions so there will be absolutely no talking and definitely no getting out of seats.' I instructed them to go to their tables, row by row.

Once they were sat down, I administered the correct tests to the right pupils and they began. The door opened and in walked an adult with a girl. I assumed that this must be the teaching assistant as I'd not seen one as yet. It turned out that she wasn't the teaching assistant, she was a support worker and the girl had a hearing impairment.

'Not while they're doing the test, but when you're speaking to the whole class, you'll need to wear this head set,' said the lady. I'd worn head sets and microphones before but this one was different. Usually it was like having a Dictaphone around my neck. I tested it out to check it was working. When I spoke into it, the whole class could hear me through the speakers in the classroom. I felt like I was giving a sermon or a motivational talk and I didn't like it. I was so used to knowing the volume level of my own voice when projecting it for a whole class to hear, yet every time I spoke it was louder than I anticipated and I felt myself trailing off, in an attempt to quieten myself down.

I was suitably distracted to put the headset away when one of the children, going by the name of Ashley-Leigh, had her hand up.

'Miss, I'm stuck,' she whined.

'What's the problem?'

'It's too hard, I can't read it.'

'Do you struggle with reading?'

'Not normally, but this writing is weird.'

'What do you mean it's weird?'

'I can't read any of the letters, they look strange.' By this point I had just about fathomed the problem and I was shocked when I realised that she wasn't joking.

'Perhaps if you turn your test paper the right way up you'll be able to read it?'

'Oh, yeah!'

There was another hand in the air, this time it was Ben Drover. 'What it is, Ben?'

'I don't get it, Miss.'

'What don't you get?'

'I don't know what I've got to do.'

'Well what did it say when you read it?'

'What? You mean I've got to read it?'

'Yes! You have to actually read it!'

After that I wandered around the class at arms' length from everyone, avoiding stupid conversations like the previous two. Being an invigilator was really boring. Apart from treating the odd whisper as if it was punishable by death there was nothing much to do. Luckily, there was a catalogue on the side at the back and I decided to flick through the latest Maths games available for schools to purchase. At lunchtime I could see if they were any cheaper on Amazon.

The other Ben raised his hand, 'Miss, I need a calculator.'

'No, you can't use a calculator, Ben. It says on the front of the test, 'Non-calculator test'.'

'No really, I need one.'

'Ben, what did I just say?'

'No really, Miss, look, it says here ... calculate 52 x 36.'

'I'm not supposed to help you in any way, but it means work it out ... on paper or in your head!' Just to be sure, I then reiterated to the whole class the fact that 'calculate' did not mean that you could only use a calculator to work it out.

Stephanie had her hand up, 'Miss, I've finished.' That was quick.

'Have you checked it?

'No,' and she began flicking through the pages. Now, I know that children are not taught to check tests by flicking through the pages of their test without actually reading anything, so why is it that they all do it, no matter who they are, whatever school or area they are from? Perhaps the problem is that most of them are not taught to check their tests at all and really see the exercise as something the teacher tells you to do when you've finished because they can't think of anything else, which in a way, is also true!

'Stephanie, to check your work you have to read each question again and work it out again to see if your answer is right.'

'Aww Miss, that'll take ages!'

'Yes it will, but it could mean the difference between getting a level three or a level four, so it is well worth doing.' She set to work but I was sure that she was just staring at the pages for a longer period of time as no working out seemed to be taking place. Some of the sums even I'd struggle to do in my head.

When it was ten o'clock I gave the children their five

minute warning, 'Okay year five, you have five minutes left to finish your test.' Now for some reason, even though I'd clearly stated that there were five more minutes until the test was over, more than half of them thought that it was time to pack away and started talking to the people next to them. 'The test is not over. There should be no talking! Use this time to check your answers.' They were clearly bored so I didn't wait the whole five minutes before putting them out of their misery.

At 10:07am we lined up and began the long walk to the assembly hall. As I led the line down the corridor I was quite pleased that they weren't making too much racket. We passed classrooms, work areas and corridors veering off to the right. Periodically, I checked behind me to see if anyone was up to terrible mischief. After we'd passed the third corridor veering off the right I peered behind me and was shocked to see Stephanie at the front of the line and the rest of the children being held up behind her. She was at least twenty paces behind me.

'What's the matter, Stephanie?' I questioned.

'It's this way, Miss,' she said, performing the tiniest point with her finger, arm still by her side while she pointed to the corridor. More embarrassment. I'm so used to it that it's just water off a duck's back. Supply teaching is probably the easiest job to appear incompetent in, even when you're good at it.

'Oops, sorry,' I muttered. I then chose to follow her instead, the rest of the way to assembly.

In the assembly hall, the whole school had gathered from nursery, all the way through to year six and we were as usual, the last class to take our places. The assembly was as boring as ever, and were it not for the fact I was sat on the most uncomfortable bench that was so low my knees were up to my ears, I might have nodded off. Just as I thought it was over they began giving out awards. That usually takes ages! When there were about ten children stood at the front with their awards, I witnessed the strangest thing that was almost unbelievable and it's likely I'll never see it again. A small, black cat trotted in from the cloakroom, situated at the front of the hall. Most of the children noticed it before the head teacher did and they began chattering and nudging each other. One of the nursery children cried out, screaming whilst the others leant forward for a stroke and the cat obliged quite happily. What followed next was most intriguing.

'Whose is this cat?' bellowed Mr Thorn. There was no reply. 'It must be somebody's! Whose is it?!' Still no reply. He picked the cat up by the scruff of the neck, as its mother would do, and began walking towards the door. It was at that point a girl of about five or six jumped to her feet.

'Get off my cat! You're hurting my cat!' she shouted angrily. Boy, she was going to be in trouble. Mr Thorn signalled for her to follow him with his long, bony finger, which she did nervously, and the three of them exited the room. No more was said on the matter and to my delight, the presentation of awards was abandoned and the children were dismissed calmly outside for playtime. I skipped back to the classroom to collect my coat for the duty I had to cover.

Later in the day I followed up on the cat incident. It turned out that the girl had encouraged the cat to follow her to school, which apparently it did on a regular basis. On this occasion though, it followed her inside and after she'd been to the toilets next to the cloakroom the cat was still there so she decided to bundle the cat up and put it inside her pump bag with her PE kit. The cat must have found it quite comfortable for over an hour until it heard everyone in the hall and went in search of the attention.

Out in the playground, I was the only adult as usual until seven minutes in. I've got to the point where I can predict this sort of stuff happening before it does and it always makes me chuckle. I stood in one position that had a wide view of the playground until a few little sheep came up behind me. I started off in another direction and stopped after a few paces, then they followed. It was like being in a really slow relay race.

'Girls ... have you not got anything better to do?'

They looked at each other and then at me, 'No.'

'Hmm, I'm sure you do. I'm not a shepherd you know and you are not sheep.'

'Eh?'

'Oh never mind.'

'So ... are you a new teacher?'

'Well, I'm here today, but year five's teacher will be back soon.'

'So which class are you going to be the teacher of?'

'I'm not. I'm just here for the day.'

'Why?'

'Because I like going to lots of different schools and meeting different children.'

'Oh. So are you a supply teacher?'

'Yes.' I usually tried to avoid admitting that to the children, almost as if by doing so it gave them the go-ahead to behave like idiots.

'So don't you want to be a real teacher?'

'I am a real teacher. I tell you what girls, why don't you see who can get to that wall at the other side of the playground first? On your marks, get set, go.' That was an ingenious way I liked to employ to get rid of them. Off they sped. I walked to a different area of the playground, where the boys were playing football, to avoid another encounter with them. I took my life in my own hands as I stood on the side lines.

'Miss, do it again.' It was those two again!

'Ah girls, you found me. Why don't you go and play somewhere?'

'Don't want to. Miss, how old are you?' That old chestnut again.

'I'm one hundred and seven.'

'Really? That old? Have you got false teeth?' False teeth! Cheeky or what?

'No, I've looked after my teeth very well.'

'I thought they'd have fallen out by now.'

'On your marks, get set, go.' Anything for a bit of peace, and off they sped again.

One of the other adults made their way over to me. 'I thought it was Mrs Farrar's duty today, I'm sure I've seen her in school.'

'Oh, it probably was, but Mr Jones obviously wanted to get out of his duty this week so he swapped so it'd be his duty when he was out.'

'He seems to do that a lot. I think I've only seen him do three duties this year.' She wandered off now she had her snippet of gossip and the two girls were waiting patiently to quiz me again.

'Miss, are you Mr Jones' friend?' They were back again.

'Yes, I know him.' I hated lying. I was definitely going

to trip myself up at some point.

'What's his dog called then?'

'I've never met his dog.'

'Well he loves his dog and if you're *really* his friend you should know his name.'

'Well I might have heard it before but I've just forgotten. Why don't you tell me his dogs name and then I might remember it.' I was hopeful that would work.

'He's called Clarkson.'

'After Jeremy Clarkson?'

'Who?'

'On Top Gear.'

'No, he said he named him after his favourite car program.' It was beginning to sound like this was a guy I would actually get on with.

'Exactly.'

'Miss...'

'On your marks, get set, go!' They were off again, a little break before they started their next line of enquiry.

'Are you Mr Jones's girlfriend?'

'No, I'm married to Mr Harley.'

'Yeah, but you can have a wife and a girlfriend.'

'Can you?' We do our best to deny all notions of immorality, in the hope that we will partake in the creation of good citizens.

'My Dad has a girlfriend and my mum is his wife.'

It was the head teacher that came out to blow the whistle and I was relieved that I had been saved from any further difficult conversation. It occurred to me that the adults may not have been trusted to decide when playtime was over or to get them organised lining up. As a head teacher, he did possess a 'presence' which in this day and age is becoming more and more rare. His existence in the playground did change the children's behaviour, which was win-win for me, angling for an easy life.

Back in the classroom, I sat the children down on the carpet and then remembered that the laptops were needed for the lesson. Thus far, no teaching assistant had set foot in the room and the hearing impaired girl with her support worker had not returned to our classroom after break time. I puzzled over how I was going to get the laptops for a few moments.

'Nathan.' He stood up, willingly. The changed child syndrome had not worn off and so I took the opportunity to fuel the fire before it died out. 'Remember that massive favour you did for me earlier?' He nodded. 'Could you take a message next door again?' He was more than happy to get out of class for a few minutes and feel important. I wrote a note for the neighbouring teacher, explaining our difficulty. Her solution baffled me somewhat. It turned out that she had a teaching assistant (I'd begun to think that they didn't exist in this school). Instead of doing what I would consider 'the sensible thing' by sending the teaching assistant for the laptop trolley for our class, she sent the teaching assistant in to watch the class so that I could go get the laptop trolley.

After spending five minutes looking for the library where they were kept I realised why. There was a big sign on the library door saying, 'Notice to Staff: All Laptop trolleys must be signed out by teachers only. Laptops are your responsibility when signed out by you and any damage or theft will be investigated.' Were it not for the fact that I'd disturbed the other class and didn't have anything else planned, with no teaching assistant to do any relevant photocopying, I may have just left them alone. No-one wants to sign their life away when they see a notice like that, especially when you know that they are going to be handled by nine and ten year olds whom you don't really know and who are also likely to try it on with an unknown member of staff.

I signed the book in the presence of the librarian, who opened the trolley with a key and placed it back in the drawer where she'd got it from, under the monitor. I began dragging the heavy laptop trolley down the corridor, stopping every few steps to try and straighten up again. Its unruly back wheels were making life very difficult.

On arrival at the classroom, I tried to open the door with one hand and pull the trolley through with the other but it was too heavy. Then I tried swinging the door open wide and pushing the trolley through the door before it closed but I wasn't quick enough. All the while the teaching assistant from next door just sat there, not lifting a finger or even instructing a child to help.

'Nathan!' I called into the class. He'd help me. He shuffled over and I had him pull whilst I pushed. We got it moving and heard a thud, the trolley would not move any more. On closer inspection, it was actually too big for the door! Talk about delayed, the teaching assistant then chipped in.

'Oh they are too big to fit through the doors so you'll have to keep it on the corridor. Anyway, I best get back to my own class,' she said as she came towards us and squeezed through the tiniest gap, despite being on the heavy side, rather than waiting for us to move it out of the way.

I instructed the students, one by one, to collect a

laptop, feeling thinly spread as I straddled the doorway, trying desperately to be superwoman and have my eyes everywhere, in the classroom as well as on the corridor. When every child had a laptop, there were still three laptops left in the trolley but I had no key to lock it, despite signing them out in my name. Their red lights were blinking, informing me that they were charging, and I could see how that could be potentially beneficial given my many previous experiences with these blasted things. I considered leaving it to chance, but it would have only taken one thieving little toe-rag passing by for it all to go pear-shaped. I decided prevention was the best option and moved them into the classroom.

It was a good job that they didn't need any input to get on with the research as I'd lost all access to the teacher's computer again. I didn't bother disturbing next door. I just managed without it for a while.

I seized the day whilst the children were working relatively quietly to make a start on the Maths tests. I picked out the most troublesome table and sat at that one in the hope that my presence would calm them into submission. I then began checking the answers, this time with purple and orange pens, which I'd had to borrow from Mr Jones' desk as they're not exactly common pen colours. It was part of the school marking policy. Correct answers had to be marked in purple while incorrect answers were marked in orange. What a farce! It took twice as long just swapping the pens around and every two minutes I was checking the marking policy again because I couldn't remember which was for which.

Nathan was sat on my table and obviously, in his opinion, I was sat there because I wanted nothing more than to have a lovely chat with him and his friends. It's quite hard to follow a marking scheme and mark with two different pens whilst counting the child's score in your head at the same time in order to avoid having to look through the paper for a second time at the end. I humoured him, as after all, I wanted to keep him on side and he had been rather helpful that morning.

'My sister's just had a baby,' he said proudly.
'That's nice, so are you an uncle now then?'
'Yes, I'm Uncle Nathan.'
'What's the baby called?'
'Jordan.'
'So have you got a niece or a nephew?'
'No, it's a baby.'
'Yes, I know that. Is it a boy or a girl?'
'I don't know, when I saw it, it was wearing yellow.'
'Perhaps that's something you could find out tonight then.'

I looked over the marking scheme again, purple for right and orange for wrong. Oh great! The last three papers I'd done whilst small talking were the wrong way around, all the ticks were orange and all the dots (yes dots, not crosses – too negative apparently, like red pen) were purple. I proceeded to spend another four minutes correcting them all. Nathan continued to chat at me, so with those papers corrected I began meandering around the room again to escape.

It wasn't long before I had the first complaint of a laptop running out of battery power. I swapped it with one of the three reserves I'd brought in earlier. One down, two to go. Five minutes later and we'd lost another one. Two down, one to go. A minute after that we lost two at the same time and there was only one spare left. I hadn't finished sorting that when four more conked out. What a nightmare!

'Okay year five, if you have a laptop that no longer works, partner up with someone whose laptop does work. There were about five more minutes of shuffling around, chair migration and minor arguments which they relayed to me in detail along the lines of, 'She's annoying me with her chair, there's no room for it,' or 'He won't let me work with him,' or 'I'm not working with her, she's a geek,' and 'He's hogging the laptop.' Just as I'd done the rounds on the petty problems and the agro was about to feel 'worth it' for the extra occupied time I'd regained, all the remaining laptops shut down within 30 seconds of each other. It was like someone had turned the power off, except they weren't plugged in.

Chatter filled the classroom which quickly escalated to a rowdy din. It was 11:15am and there were still thirty minutes of Literacy to kill.

I raised my voice, 'Right year five, let's have everybody listening and looking this way in five, four, three, two, one.' At that point, I had no idea what my next move would be, but waiting an extra-long time after every little disturbance, such as muttering, gave me more time to think about it.

'You didn't forget, Miss, you only counted from five,' interrupted Nathan. It took me a moment to realise what an earth he was going on about, but the shouting out had annoyed me, especially as I'd just got the attention of the whole class. There's knowing when it's appropriate and when it's not. He didn't seem to know. The cross look I gave him said a thousand words and I continued.

'You are going to take your laptop to the laptop trolley …' they started grabbing for the laptops and nudging each other out of the way, '... have I finished giving the instruction?' It was a rhetorical question, however, I received an answer. That happens to me lot and I never seem to learn.

'No Miss,' blurted Ben. The best option was to ignore him.

'Don't do anything until I've given you all of the instructions. You're going to put your laptop back in the trolley when I tell you to and make sure it's plugged in. Then you're going to go to your guided reading tables and read quietly until everyone is ready. Understood?'

Heads were bobbing up and down all around the room. I let them return their laptops a table at a time. The plan was to get the teaching assistant from next door back to get rid of them and out of my care as soon as possible. Once they'd all returned them, I did a count up, just to check they were all there. I could hear them chattering away to each other very loudly. I raced back into the classroom.

'I'm only in the corridor, I can hear you. I want to hear silence.' The volume decreased considerably, it wasn't silence, but for the meantime, I was happy with it. I dashed back out to the corridor and counted up, still all present and correct. This time I sent Ben next door as Nathan had seemingly become confused and thought that we had achieved 'friend status'. It turned out that she was running a reading group and I'd have to wait fifteen minutes. It was at this point that a key would have been just the ticket.

The next errand I sent Ben on was to get the key from the library so that we could lock the trolley. Waiting for him to return I repeated the same routine. Walking around the class once and then checking the laptops were still there and then I went through the rigmarole again. If I didn't check the laptops, they'd probably go walkabouts and if I didn't walk around the class, the noise level got too loud.

When Ben returned, he told me that the lady was not allowed to give the laptop trolley key to a supply teacher. Interesting. So, for the next half an hour I'd have to leave the laptops vulnerable if I wanted to do any work with the class because I had no teaching assistant. Out of curiosity, I asked Ben where the teaching assistant was.

'She never comes in when we have a supply teacher, Mr Jones gives her loads of stuff to do for all the walls.'

'So, do you have a supply teacher often then?'

'He has a lot of meetings and then we get a supply teacher or Mrs Ansell.' I put two and two together and figured Mrs Ansell was the PPA teacher. If Mr Jones did the same rigmarole with every supply teacher, he'd have an awful lot of make-believe friends. I resigned myself to the fact that I was going to have to relax a little on the crime watch front and check the trolley every five minutes or so.

Albeit early, the class needed to be getting on as they were losing the will to live, as was I, and so I started the treacherously long guided reading session fifteen minutes early, in the hope that the last 15 minutes before lunchtime could be spent playing a game if they behaved well - this was also a good bribe.

I started with the clever group, my theory being that they could manage to get on with whatever I'd asked for a minute or so every time I needed to check the laptops. I started with Madeline on my left and they all read a page each. To be fair, they were extremely patient with the constant interruptions and me having to address the whole class asking them to be quiet. The thing that I hate about guided reading is that you are with this one group and really concentrating on what they are doing, saying and trying to assess them while all the other kids know you can't really see what they're doing and you're not available to check up on them. Forty-five minutes of that is hell in my eyes!

It was time to check on the laptops. My stomach started churning at the unbelievable discovery. There were two missing. I'd been shoved unwillingly into this situation in the first place and was unclear about the potential repercussions. The class volume control had turned itself way up and I dashed back in to have a go at them.

'I am trying to sort out a very serious issue year five! Two of the laptops have gone missing!' That was sobering, there were gasps and whispered that followed and I made my way out onto the corridor again. Three missing! How was this happening? I counted them again to check I wasn't going mad, even though I could clearly see the empty shelves.

A year six boy came out of his classroom and removed another laptop from its shelf.

'Excuse me, what do you think you're doing?' I asked angrily.

'I'm taking these laptops into our classroom,' he replied with no ounce of remorse.

'And why are you doing that? They are signed out for year five. Besides, all the batteries have died.'

'My teacher told me to do it and we have chargers in our class because we're year six.' Flipping year six teachers, again! I marched over to her classroom door.

'Excuse me,' I yelled through the doorway, not waiting for her to pause what she was doing before continuing. 'I've had to sign these laptops out in my name and I have no key to lock the trolley. I'm not happy about you taking them.'

'Well these are year six children and we need to make all the resources available to them in the short time they have with us to ensure their maximum potential is reached in the coming months. At the moment, these resources are available and are not being used by your class so we'll be using them instead.' What could I say to that? Trumped, yet again by the year six SATs card.

I couldn't concentrate on the reading as I was too busy worrying about the laptops being in the care of the somewhat blasé year six teacher but still under my responsibility. The interruptions were driving me crazy, and half of those were the whole class interruptions I was having to make myself to shut the rest of the class up. Whoever's idea it was to have effectively two guided reading sessions straight after each other was an idiot! It was now 11:45am, time for guided reading to officially begin and I was already fed up with it, quarter of an hour in.

At that moment, Sammy, the hearing impaired girl and her support worker arrived. It seemed they were joining us for the guided reading session. They sat at our table and she handed me the headset. With it on, I began teaching the reading group. My voice boomed over the sound system which made the other children talk even louder to get a word in edge ways over it. I'd had enough.

'Right year five, that is enough!' I yelled, shocking the children to attention and scaring myself a bit with the volume coming out of the speakers. I quietened down, 'There will be no more talking from any group that is not working with me. Silence.'

'Why is it golden, Miss?' Nathan shouted out.

'Not now, Nathan! Not now!' I slid back into my chair and continued. Luckily, after a while I got used to the headset and at times I even forgot I was wearing it. Another agonising fifteen minutes passed before I gave up the ghost and told the whole class we were playing *heads down, thumbs up*. There were cheers, stretched bodies and fingers pointing to the sky.

Despite leading the game vocally and needing to remember all the names in the class I managed to mark ninety per cent of the remaining Maths tests before lunch, with the correct coloured pens too.

The dinner lady showed up five minutes early which was an unusual bonus, only to shatter their dreams by informing them that it was indoor play. I hated wet play too, especially at lunch times. I decided at that point to slip out to the toilet so I could get the rest of the tests marked before setting out on my next adventure and hopefully I'd have spare time for lunch in the very short forty-minute lunch break. I complain when it's too long and I've nothing to do and then I complain when it's too short and there's lots to do. I'm probably never happy.

To get to the toilet I had to pass through the dining hall, where key stage one were already having their lunch. As a rule, key stage one children are not afraid to approach strangers, especially in school.

'Are you a new teacher?' asked a red haired girl, knelt up on her chair.

'I'm just here for the day.'

'Are you going to come and teach our class?'

'No, I don't think so. I only do the older ones.'

'Aww, that's not fair.' At which point the boy next to her made the most interesting comment.

'Look Miss, I'm a bender.'

'Pardon? You're a bender?'

'Yes, look, I'm a bender, a bender of spoons,' he said as he changed the shape slightly of the cheap teaspoon he'd brought in from home.

'I don't think the adult at home will be pleased when they find out you've been bending spoons.'

'No, she won't mind. She's knows I'm a bender.' I just smiled politely and escaped the conversation.

It appeared that I'd arrived at the ladies at the right time as they were empty. I peered in the first one.

'Oh that's disgusting!' Someone had been previously and not flushed it. The next toilet was satisfactory and I went in, did my business and started singing, as you do, despite the fact it was Thursday, 'I'm so excited ... and I just cat hide it ... I'm about to lose control and I think I ...' then I heard someone come in. In fact there were two people and they were in the middle of a loud conversation.

'Didn't you think it was obvious?'

'No, I'd never have put them two together.'

'I could see it bubbling for weeks.'

'Do you think they'll get married?'

'Mr and Mrs Jones ... I suppose anything is possible.'

'Surely the head can't be impressed that they're both in year five. It's not exactly condoned to start going out with your year group partner.'

'Do any of the kids know?'

'Oh no, we best keep that one under our belts. Can you imagine the scandal if the children found out that Mr Jones and Miss Steeple were boyfriend and girlfriend and expecting a baby. They'd never hear the end of it!'

'They're having a baby?!'

'Me and my big gob! I always forget to say what I'm allowed to say and what I'm not.'

'How far on is she?'

'Only eight weeks, it's early days yet.'

'Eight weeks ... nobody should know at this stage. Poor girl.'

As I flushed the toilet the voices turned to a whisper, I don't know why they were suddenly bothered. I expected to greet them as I emerged so I could put voices to faces but they were both conveniently in cubicles.

Back in class, I made a beeline for the Maths tests to get them out of the way. The dinner lady was supervising another class, washing their hands, while year five went wild. Ashley approached me, obviously hoping I'd entertain her in my lunch time.

'What is it?' I asked, surprising myself when my voice was heard through the speakers again.

'What's a bender?' Was this coincidence or was there something sinister underlying? 'A bender, what is it?'

'Why are you asking me that question?' I immediately removed the headset, fearing the worst.

'Because you were talking to a boy about a bender.'

Uh oh. This was bad, really bad. I could no longer hear myself so I assumed that it had gone off. Surely, the toilet would have been out of range.

'What else did you hear?'

'Um ... we heard you saying the toilet was disgusting and then you had a wee and then you started singing ...'

'Oh no ... how embarrassing!'

'No, you're actually quite a good singer.'

'Not that! Oh, never mind!'

'And then Miss Dean said about Mr Jones and Miss Steeple being boyfriend and girlfriend and that she's having a baby. That's when everyone giggled.'

'Everyone?'

'Yes we were all here and it went quiet because everyone wanted to listen.'

'Can you do me a favour?'

'Yeah.'

'Can you go around the class and tell everyone it's a big secret and they can't talk about it until tomorrow?'

'Okay, why?'

'Just because ... er ... it will really upset Mr Jones.'

'Okay then.' It was as simple as that. I could add this school to my list of 'no go's' at 3:15pm.

It wasn't long before Ben was at my side, yielding his Literacy book. 'Miss, I'm writing a story. It's about the war.'

'Very good, Ben, well done.'

'Look at my plan, Miss,' he said, thrusting the book right under my nose so I had no choice but to look at it.

'Yes, very good.'

'You haven't even read it.'

'I have, it's good.'

'What's it about then?'

'The war.'

'But what about the war?'

'Okay, I'll read it, but I have to be quick.' On further glance, it wasn't the story that caught my attention, it was the story mountain he'd planned his story on. It was a teacher created resource and he'd put his ideas in the relevant boxes. They were titled, 'Begining,' 'Build-up,' 'Problem,' 'Rezolution,' and 'Ending'. Mr Jones had a more serious problem than I had first thought.

As there were only fifteen minutes left of lunchtime to eat food and find out what I was doing, I left the remaining few Maths tests, it was unacceptable that he'd asked me to do them in the first place and I left at note for him describing our antics that morning. I did not mention his pending fatherhood or his relationship with the teacher next door. If the worst happened, I'd deny it.

Before I could cart my bag with everything in it but the kitchen sink with me through the classroom door, Nathan blocked my path.

'Mrs Harley,' he said, with a stern police detective look on his face.

'Yes, Nathan.'

'So, you say you are friends with Mr Jones?'

'Er ... yes.'

'And you have known him for a while?'

'Yes.'

'And you know his sister, Emily?'

'Er ...'

'You either do or you don't?'

'Y ... yes, I do.'

'So you also know that she lives in Australia.'

'Oh yes, of course.'

'Oh Miss, you've been busted! We knew you didn't know him because Mr Jones always says the supply teachers are his friends, but then he never knows their names. Mr Jones doesn't even have a sister!'

'Ah. Caught red handed. Oh well, never mind. Bye.' I

scooted around him and headed for the corridor.

THURSDAY AFTERNOON

I'd been waiting at the reception desk for seven minutes when I decided to get an egg sandwich out of my bag and devour it. It was unfortunate for the interview candidates sat to my right, but there were only ten minutes of lunchtime left. They all looked like they were newly qualified teachers anyway, so a smelly egg sandwich wouldn't have put them off, all desperate to prove that they could get their first job. The office staff were still trying to figure out where best to place me that afternoon. I even volunteered to go home, despite the fact that I would have found that quite annoying, after already spending so much extra time at the school and missing out on the half-day luxury of a hot lunch at home. With what was about to transpire, it would have certainly been the easiest option. They didn't grant me that though, instead, they decided that the time should be spread out equally among the key stage two staff. Mr Jones was having his PPA anyway, so he didn't count, and the year six teachers were so important that they got extra PPA every afternoon, so that left five teachers.

The afternoon was two hours and five minutes long or a hundred and twenty-five minutes for calculation purposes. This gave each teacher twenty-five minutes out of class to do goodness knows what, and at that moment in time, they had no idea about it. At this point, I was just glad that they hadn't come up with a really obscure number, like twenty-three and a half as I'm convinced they would have made me uphold that in the nature of fairness. I'm sure you can imagine how helpful a teacher would find it to be told to leave their classroom for twenty-five minutes mid-lesson when they had no intention of passing it onto someone else.

She scrawled out a timetable on a piece of scrap paper and handed it to me. I ate my other sandwich on the way to the classroom, it was year three.

There were two minutes to go until the bell when I arrived and the teacher was not there. I had no idea what she looked like either, in fact, it could have been a man. It wasn't as if I could come up with my own thing when the teacher was going to be teaching most of the afternoon. When the bell did sound and no one had showed up I returned to the pick-up point from the morning where I'd collected the year five class, hoping the teacher would be waiting out there.

I made my way down the line of teachers, asking them if they were the teacher of this particular year three class and of course I ended up asking everyone as it was the last person in the line that I needed. She was very surprised as she had no knowledge of it.

'What? Now?'

'Yes, I know it's short notice, but it's what they've decided. I just do as I'm told.'

'Yes, sorry, I can appreciate that. I've … er …

planned a detailed art activity for this afternoon so I'll need to start them off.'

'Yes, that's fine, in fact, that would be useful as we've had no time to talk anything through.'

'Hmm,' she agreed. 'How long did you say it was for again?'

'Twenty-five minutes.'

'Right.'

The children in the year three class were beginning to get restless and we both noticed.

'Right year...' we both said in unison and I trailed off in embarrassment. 'Sorry,' I said and let her continue. It was difficult being a glorified teaching assistant.

'Right year three, I'm looking for smart children ready to walk quietly back to class.'

They were an okay bunch. They were not really naughty or malicious, but I felt that the teacher could have had higher expectations. She'd said she wanted smart children, but then set off anyway. She tolerated more chatter and noise than I would have and I found myself itching to say something on several occasions on the way back to class. I fought the urge.

Once in the classroom, children sat at desks, she took the register. It was now 1:15pm and so five minutes of her twenty-five minute slot had already been wasted on the journey to the classroom. There was an underlying murmur while she carried out the roll call and I marched around the class like Hitler, trying to seek out those who were talking and scowling at them. By the time she'd finished that it was 1:18pm. The timetable was ridiculous and I imagined it would only get worse as the afternoon progressed.

The teacher, Miss Wood, had everyone gather

around the biggest table so she could show them the art activity and they could see what she was doing. The task was lengthy and involved a very messy process. I have to admit, I was glad I was not scheduled to be part of the clean-up operation. In all honesty, had I been set this piece of work to do for the full lesson, I'd probably have tried to find a way to get out of it. There's nothing worse than a load of paper everywhere and no idea where to put it!

After a little pushing and shoving from some of the children trying to get a better view, Miss Wood began. She was making a 3D model of the classroom. The children had designed ideal classrooms and had to work from their plan. She painstakingly showed them how to make each piece of furniture out of card, paint it up and add decoration. By the end of her demonstration, she'd showed them one table, one chair, a bookcase, a wardrobe and how to cover the floor with tissue paper. It was now 1:30pm and she'd actually rushed through the input.

'Right, I'll leave you to it, Miss ...?' she called, reaching for the door.'

'Harley, Mrs Harley,' I replied, sounding like a broken record to myself.

'See you in twenty-five.'

'Erm, actually, five.'

'What?!'

'I've to be in year four in five minutes, it's been spread out equally.'

'You're joking! What was the point? Why don't they tell us these things?'

'Best take it up with the office,' I called out to her as she made her way down the long corridor.

I could understand her frustration. If they'd have sorted it out sooner, they could have consulted the staff and perhaps placed me in a classroom that was reading independently for the first twenty-five minutes.

I wandered around the anarchy whilst every child fought over the pieces of card and decoration materials. There'd been no instructions left on handing any of the materials out, she'd just let them go for it, and for five minutes, who was I to judge?

Five minutes soon passed with me attempting to shush the children without sincere feeling and at the same time wandering around the classroom pretending to be interested in the structures they were starting on. Covering in a class for twenty-five minutes is never a good thing. You have to buy into what you're doing. I like to know I'm going to see something through.

1:35pm arrived but Miss Wood did not. I was on a tight schedule as it was. There was no teaching assistant to take over or to find out where she was so I was stuck and I'm sure Miss Wood knew it. To be honest, if it had been me, once I'd realised I only had five minutes, I'd have probably stayed in the classroom anyway because the only useful things I'd be able to think of to get done in a five minute slot would be to go to the toilet or to make a hot drink, or perhaps both at a push. As it had only been twenty minutes since lunchtime, her coffee was probably still hot (another reason why I love travel mugs) and she'd not had time to drink it to even need the toilet again.

Five minutes later, at 1:40pm she strolled in, yes that's right, she wasn't even rushing.

'Well, I've haven't got anything done, there just wasn't enough time.'

I wasn't surprised at that remark. I just wasn't impressed at the fact I was being made to feel guilty, like it was my fault. I didn't have time to chat so I just responded with a weak smile and tried to find my way to the next class. I stopped and asked for directions on two occasions. Here was yet another flaw in the timetable, the year four class I was going to was at the other side of the school so I was now almost ten minutes late, not that the teacher would have known. I was faced with a dilemma. It was now 1:45pm and there were one and a half hours left to be shared between four teachers. Should I bin one of them off and give only three teachers thirty minutes? Or I could give the next teacher ten minutes less and then go back to agreed schedule? Alternatively, I could share the ninety minutes between the four teachers and give them all twenty two and a half minutes each.

Some may say it was not my decision to make, but if I hadn't have taken on the challenge alone, it would have involved another trek down to reception, wasting even more precious minutes. And after all, I may only be a lowly supply teacher, but I'm still a professional who is still technically capable of professional judgement. Honest. I considered the options carefully, and, in all my wisdom, concluded that it would be better to share the time out equally but to tell the teachers that they only had twenty minutes, thus, giving me a little leeway should they return late. Genius.

On arrival at the year four classroom, I interrupted the children putting their things away and sitting on the carpet. Great. A new activity again.

'I'm here to give you twenty minutes out of class,' I told the large, stern faced teacher.

'Who's said this then?' she asked fiercely.

'I've been given the instructions by the ladies in the office.'

'Which ladies?'

'Well, I don't know the school, or them.' Her eyes narrowed and I racked my brain to give her some morsel of information to prove I was telling the truth. I was beginning to think I should have binned off the time this teacher had. 'The main one had short brown hair?'

She nodded in recognition.

'I think she was wearing a blue top too.'

'And she's only given me twenty minutes?' she scowled.

'Yes I'm afraid so, due to the first teacher being a little delayed.'

'But I'm just about to start them off on a new activity.'

'Could I make a suggestion?'

She glared at me, but I took it as a nod.

'Perhaps you will get the most out of your time if we read independently for twenty minutes while you get some things done, otherwise you may end up losing some of your time too.'

'They've just finished thirty minutes of guided reading. Besides, by the sounds of it, I've already had some time shaved off anyway!'

'Er ... yes, but it's very marginal, a few minutes, that's all.'

She sat on the large bucket chair at the front of the carpet area, her cheeks overhanging on either side. For the next ten minutes, she proceeded to read them a story – surely, something I could have done. Their task was to act out one of the scenes. There were no special key words she'd used or vocabulary that they needed to include that I was too thick to understand. I sat there baffled, on a hard chair next to the carpet, wondering why I was playing the role of glorified teaching assistant when this teacher was wasting so much time. She let them choose their own groups (a disaster in my eyes) and headed for the door.

After the last teacher's antics, I dared to be cheeky. 'See you back in ten minutes then.'

'Ten? I thought it was twenty!'

'Yes, but it started from the moment I walked in the room, everyone else needs their turn too.'

She walked off without saying anything.

Year four's drama skills were not very good. If there's one thing I like to be a little bit serious about, it's drama. Everyone has their 'thing' and drama is one of mine. I like to see the facial expressions and well thought out stage directions. I can't stand it when pupils have acted it out once and tell me they've finished. It was the case in this class.

'Miss, we've finished,' whined three girls in a group together with no male group member. This mystified me somewhat as the piece had five characters, two males and three females. It was the same story as I looked around the room. One group had seven boys in it, but it wasn't as if I could change that now, the teacher had set it up and she was coming back to finish it, hopefully, in the not too distant future.

'You can't possibly have finished. A piece of drama is never finished,' I said, going all thespian on them, RP (Received Pronunciation) accent coming through sarcastically.

'Why are you talking funny?'

'Never mind.' My humour was lost on them. 'Show me what you have already.' They did. It was rubbish. And I mean, really bad. It consisted of three words that only one girl said while they all stood there, frozen to the spot, not facing the audience. 'How about we change it so everyone has a speaking part?' It wasn't as if I was allowed to tell them it was rubbish blatantly, instead, I had to choose clever words to tell them it was rubbish, kind of like walking on eggshells.

The one who had done all the speaking so far answered, 'No Miss, they can't, they don't know how to talk.'

'In real life, or in the play?'

'Well that's a silly thing to say, in the play of course.' Perhaps she didn't know it was possible. I've learnt the hard way never to take anything for granted.

'Okay. I don't remember that being in the story that our teacher read out.'

'Yeah, but we've changed the characters. Miss lets us.' And there it was, that terrible phrase, 'Miss lets us'. In normal circumstances I'd have challenged that greatly, but as there were only a few minutes to her return, I ignored it.

'What about some movement? Perhaps these two girls could be doing something while you're speaking. Maybe they could be sat at the table, pretending to have a cup of coffee.'

'No Miss, they can't move. All their joints have gone stiff.'

'And is this part of their character's too?' If only they'd have put as much creativity into their actual drama piece that they were using now just to get out of improving what they'd already done.

'Yeah, Miss lets us.'

'I see. Well what about you getting up and putting a bit of action into it?'

'No Miss, it's fine how it is. We normally only do it once. Miss lets us.' Annoyed at the repetition, I gave up and made my way to the group with the seven boys.

I glanced up at the clock, it was 2:04pm. The teacher was expected back in one minute. I had a feeling that she wasn't going to stick to the timetable and so I continued with the boys regardless.

'Right boys, show me what you have so far.' It was better than the girl's piece, but not by much. At least everyone said something, even if it was, 'wah' like the too smallest boys did, pretending to be twin babies, and no, there were no babies in the story either. They all seem to have this obsession with having a baby in the play, it's almost like they are re-creating playing 'mums and dads' in the key stage one playground. In fact, that's the nearest some of them have ever got to drama. Many can't even say that they've seen a really bad puppet show or rip off musical, usually performing in a theme park or zoo. So it's not like they had much to go on.

The challenge here was finding just one thing to work on in the short time that we had, without making them feel like they were completely useless. I'm not exactly known for brilliant tact, or telling people they are brilliant when they clearly are not, but I gave it a go.

'It's a good start, boys, everybody is saying something. I think we can improve it though.'

'Aww, Miss,' moaned one of the 'baby twins'. 'We've done it now. We don't want to make it better.'

'Well your teacher isn't back yet, even though she should be, so let's make the most of the time we've got.'

Pretty much all of them started grumbling.

'Let's start at the beginning and go through it line by line and see if we're all stood in the right places. This is actually called blocking. I used to be a drama teacher you know.'

'Blocking? Like with Lego, but bigger?'

'Well no, I know it sounds a bit like that, but it means deciding what your position is in different parts of the script, and having a reason for being there.'

'Oh right, I get it.' He didn't sound convinced.

'Get into the places that you're in at the beginning.'

They did that, most of them were in exactly the same position they were in at the end. The most amusing part about it was that the story was about poor people taking a journey across America in the 1800's yet no one seemed to want to do any walking. They began.

'I'm running up mountain,' said the boy pretending to be the grandfather.

'Me too,' said the person pretending to be the grandmother.

'Okay, stop, stop, stop.'

'But Miss, I haven't done my bit yet!' said the boy playing the father.

'Yes, alright, but we've a few things to sort out first.' I had no idea which issue to broach first. Which was more pressing? The fact that they were stating that they were running up a mountain and no one in their right mind would say that naturally, or the fact they were stood still while doing it, or the fact they were supposed to be very elderly and incapable of doing what they were saying? The whole speaking with a northern English accent thing to boot, well, that had to be brushed under the carpet. 'Do you think it might be a good idea to pretend that the grandparents are in a wagon, or are being helped along by some of the younger people?'

'Aww Miss, we don't wanna change it now. It's finished.' It was like talking to a brick wall and they were not making themselves easy to direct.

I glanced at the clock again, surely, at least a minute had passed. It was now 2:15pm and the teacher was ten minutes late.

'I'll tell you what, boys, you have a think about what I've said because you're not going to be given anything else to do while I'm here, your drama needs to improve.'

I meandered over to the first group of girls and sent one of them on an errand, despite it being against school policy to send children on whole school searches. Her mission was to find her teacher.

Another five minutes later the girl returned with a verbal, not even written, message.

'Miss says to tell you that she's spoken to the office and they said it's okay for her to have extra time. She said, *If the class are getting bored then you can get them to show what they've done.*'

'Right...' I had only her word to go on, but it was the only word I had so I continued on. I now had even less idea about how the afternoon was going to unfold. I didn't know how long this 'extra time' was going to be.

Most of the class had absolutely no interest in improving their work and showing them to the class was going to take all of five minutes as the average piece was fifteen seconds long. This was actually surprising, as usually, you get at least one group who don't know when to end and they keep going on, and on, and on, and on, despite making several attempts to stop them. The usual line is, 'Oh Miss, we've just got this next bit,' and then they carry on covering the same ground all over again. Maybe I should have been thankful that there would be none of that.

The boys group was first to perform. The girls in the class were your typical giggly girls and they thought every line that the boys delivered was hilarious, much to my disappointment, as this encouraged them to continue their drama, on and on, unrehearsed in order to get another laugh and the worst part was, they were not even funny. I drew the line when grandma decided that she was going to do her rendition of the *Gangnam Style* to the top of the mountain.

'Okay boys, I think that's enough,' I said as I set the good example and began clapping them, albeit unenthusiastically.

I peeked at the clock again, trying not to make it obvious that I was clock watching. It was now 2:30pm. Only forty-five minutes left and three teachers to cover.

'Right, which group would like to go next?' I chose the group who had their hands up and didn't call out, how teacher-y of me. Just as they took their positions, there was a knock at the door, it was the lady with short, brown hair from the office.

'Miss … er … supply teacher,' she called. Seriously?!?! Dare I answer to that? I glared at her with raised eyebrows instead.

'Why are you still in here? The year five teacher sent her teaching assistant to look for you twenty-five minutes ago, you've completely missed her slot.'

'The teacher of this class said that she'd spoken to you and that I needed to cover in here for a longer period of time. She hasn't come back to relieve me yet. Besides, I thought the teachers didn't know.'

'Well she never asked me. You're needed elsewhere in the school, you'll have to come with me. I had to deliver some important paperwork to the next teachers classroom earlier and so I informed her of the timetable, which you haven't stuck to and now she's been without a teaching assistant for most of the afternoon!' By the way, this 'dressing down' as it were was carried out in front of the whole of the year four class. In fact, just when I hoped they'd break out into their usual loud chatter they were silent. I suppose it's like watching soaps for them, adult conversation is so scintillating because we actually know stuff that they're not supposed to know and if they're lucky, we'll slip up and they'll find out something really exciting, like me and the ladies in the toilet earlier!

'I can't leave the children unsupervised. I'll have to stay here while you sort it out.' She didn't seem too impressed with that idea.

'Have you any idea where she is?'

I pointed out the girl who had found her. The office lady had a word and then stormed off down the corridor.

She returned a few minutes later. The class and I were just chatting, after all, what was the point in trying to do anything when nobody knew for sure what was going on?

'Apparently she spoke to someone else in the office and they said that you can stay in here for the whole afternoon,' she spluttered, obviously agitated.

'The whole afternoon? I wasn't actually told a time when this stint would end, but I hadn't envisaged the whole afternoon, I was just waiting for her to come back.'

'Yes, well, you can't stay in here because you're

needed elsewhere. I'll just have to go and talk to the other woman in the office because it was not her place to go around granting extra time out of class. These are supposed to be ultimately my decisions and I am fed up of ...' and her voice trailed off down the corridor as her body went with it. One word. Communication.

2:40pm and, unsurprisingly, I was still with year four. The lady from the office returned with the other lady from the office.

'You'll have to cover them if you can't talk her round,' the brown haired lady said to the other one. 'She's your daughter.' It was all becoming clear. They disappeared for another five minutes and when they returned the class teacher was still not with them.

'Right year four,' the brown haired one addressed the whole class, 'Mrs Yardsley will be staying with you until the end of the day because Miss ... the supply teacher you've been having has to go somewhere else.'

'Mrs Yardsley? Not Miss Yardsley?' shouted one of the loud ones.

'Miss Yardsley is just getting on with some paperwork at the moment, so Mrs Yardsley will be covering.' This was just classic. If there was ever an example to the kids of how not to behave with their parents, this was it.

'Before you go, Miss ... er ... Miss, what are we supposed to be doing for the rest of the afternoon.'

'Best ask Miss Yardsley,' I replied with glee. 'We've done all the suggestions she left us.'

Her face was a picture and I actually did feel sorry for her, she'd been used and abused like me, but at least she knew about it when it was happening, unlike my oblivious self.

I grabbed my bag and walked down the corridor with the original office lady, who I now assumed must have been the head of the office, in a manner of speaking, anyway.

'So, what's the plan then?' I asked eagerly.

'Well it's 2:45pm and so that gives them ten minutes each.'

'Yeah, so which teacher are you going to choose to give the thirty minutes to?'

'I'm not, they're all going to get ten minutes each.'

'Seriously?'

'Yes. It's my decision and that's the decision I'm making.'

I really was sorry that I'd asked. We arrived at the year five class. I knew where that class was as I'd been next door all morning and the teacher had signed in for me. In fact, I knew a lot about this teacher, she had a boyfriend called Mr Jones and she was eight weeks pregnant. I probably knew more than the woman escorting me to the class, like she didn't actually trust me to get there. She knocked on the door and opened it.

'I've finally tracked down the supply teacher,' she announced triumphantly, like she deserved a medal.

'Where was she?' asked the teaching assistant. Hello! I was still there.

'Still in the year four class.' This wasn't my fault, was it? 'Anyway, she can cover you for ten minutes.'

'Ten minutes!' sneered the class teacher. 'What's the point in that?'

'Well I don't know what you want me to do about it now, it's just the way it is.'

'Well it's hardly fair is it? I was promised twenty-five minutes. Some of the other teachers have had more time.'

'Ladies,' I interjected. 'I hate to interrupt, but the fact is, while you stand here moaning and arguing about what has happened, the clock is still ticking, so unless you want to be the cause of the next two teachers getting only eight minutes each, I suggest we just get on with it.'

At first they seemed shocked by my audacity, but they quickly agreed and the office lady left.

'We're just working through the slides on the computer,' the teacher called out to me on her way out of the door. I imagined all I was doing was giving her an early toilet and coffee break, I just really didn't see the point. I'd be more useful at home now.

I sat on the comfy chair, next to the computer while the children sat on the carpet. They were doing a PSHCE lesson and on each slide was a question to discuss. I tabbed onto the next question.

'If you could be an animal, what would it be and why?' I asked the class as instructed to do by the whiteboard. It was always unnerving following someone's whiteboard presentation blind, who knew what could be on the next slide?

'Miss, weren't you in the year five class next door this morning?' one of the girls asked.

'That's right I was. But anyway, if you were an animal, what would it be?'

'Do you know Ben?'

'Which animal would it be?'

'Did you tell Ashley that Miss Dean is pregnant?'

Ground, swallow me up, now!

'I have no idea what you're talking about. Now tell me, what animal would you be?'

'Dunno.'

'Well think.'

'I don't know, Miss.'

'Anyone else?' I asked desperately, trying to move the conversation on as swiftly as possible. 'Anyone? Please, anyone? Okay. So, I think I'd be a ….' it was really hard to think on my feet, '… erm … a cow.' It was the first thing that came into my head and I regretted it the moment I'd said it.

'Eugh. Why?'

Yes, why?! Why?! 'Erm … because … they … eat grass …' totally clutching at straws, '… and … then they make milk … and … we drink … we drink the milk …' brainwave, 'so, I'd like to be a cow because I think it's very good to have a useful job in life.'

'Like teaching?'

'Yes! Exactly like teaching.' Although not the kind of teaching I was doing at that moment in time. 'Anyone else?' There was no show of hands. 'Right, we'll move on to the next question then.'

I pressed the arrow key to move along one and heard a ping. The screen was showing me the logon box. Great.

'Miss, you've got to sign in.'

'It may surprise you, but I actually do know what that means.'

'Oh, I thought you didn't because, you know, you're a supply teacher.'

'Did you know that they have computers and logon boxes like this in all the other schools?'

'Really? Not at my mum's school, she said there's no computers there.'

This was confusing, unless her mother was in sixth

form and had her daughter at age nine, this would be impossible, unless of course she was confused about college and even then, all those kind of places had computers that needed logging onto first.

'And what school does your mum go to?'

'Well she doesn't go now, silly. She went to the one down the road when she was little.' I visualised getting up and walking out, but remembered that that action would have been wrong but honestly, the temptation was still there. A little scream happened in my head which I knew I'd be able to verbalise once school had finished and that enabled me to continue.

I made a question up off the top of my head. It wasn't exactly original.

'If you were a classroom object, what would you be and why? In fact, chat to your partners about that one for thirty seconds.'

2:55pm, time for Miss Dean's return and she was on time. She peered up at the board.

'I thought you'd have got more than one question done,' she commented.

'We're on a new one now, I asked them which object they'd be and why.'

'Oh, hardly differs from an animal.'

'Well, I thought it would allow them to think of the different properties, a more, shall we say, scientific view.' There was always a way to explain away what you were doing and make it 'relevant' to the curriculum. It's a skill I've perfected over my time on supply, even if it's only to justify it to myself. 'There must be a good reason to watch this DVD'... 'It promotes an understanding of the world around them...' so on and so forth.

'She just didn't know how to logon, Miss,' shouted

the same annoying girl from earlier.

'No, it's not that I didn't know how to log on, as I explained before, I just didn't know the password.'

'That's why I told you to keep touching the whiteboard this morning, remember,' the teacher reminded me gratifyingly.

I couldn't help but bite, 'And I also recall you telling me that the children would remember to touch the board but they didn't. Anyway, I'm a minute late for my next slot now. This timetable has given no room for handover or movement.'

'Miss, that's the teacher who said you were pregnant.'

I cringed, now facing away from her. I grabbed my bag in a hurry, daring not to look back and trawled back to the other side of the building to cover the other year three class.

Now this teacher was organised. It seemed that word had got round that I'd be covering. It was probably the head office lady who went round and told them, assuming that I was going to go and hide in the toilet to get out of working or something.

'Okay, so they're reading independently,' she told me, and they were silent too. Bliss. 'Now, I know that you have to leave in ten minutes, so just listen to a few readers if you can and then Mrs Hey, the teaching assistant, is going to dismiss them at the end of the day, so just go to your next class in ten minutes and she'll sort it out from there.' Mrs Hey gave me a wave.

'How lovely, thank you,' I beamed as I sat down next to one of the children with an empty chair beside them. The teacher left the room and Mrs Hey sat down to hear a reader too. As I'd sat down, the boy next to me edged over, away from me, only a little. I seem to have that effect on children. Well, I think it's all school adults that have that effect on children. They must be worried about some kind of personal space issue or maybe they think they'll catch something, a disease that will force them to become a teacher or teaching assistant. Or worse, maybe they'll be ones to catch the nits from us! It could also be the fact they know you're about to talk to them or make them read to you and they really would rather carry on peacefully. I surprised him and asked the girl on my other side, her right side facing me, to read. He didn't see that I'd clocked it, but I noted his left fist clench slowly and his arm move in towards his body. That was unfortunate as it had just secured him the next place in my reading queue.

I appeared to have picked the top table which was ideal as they were very good readers, despite being so young, and I didn't have to correct many words. I could pretend I was listening whilst figuring what I needed to buy from the supermarket on the way home.

The time soon passed and I left the still silent class to go to the final classroom. The afternoon seemed to have gone on forever. Luckily, the last year four class was next door to the one I'd been in so I didn't have to waste any time trying to find it.

'Ah, you must be the supply teacher,' declared year four's teacher.

'That's me.'

'Right, well, we've been writing stories the whole afternoon. They can finish them off in the next seven minutes. Stop at about thirteen minutes past. There are no letters to hand out and it's not the night they take book bags home so it should be a pretty easy dismissal.'

'Do I take them somewhere to dismiss them?'

'Oh no, they're year four so they go home on their own, no need to see them out.' This was excellent news. 'Oh yes, I've left the marking policy on the desk for you for the stories.'

I chuckled, 'That's a good one!'

'A good what?'

'Joke.'

'It wasn't.'

After she'd exited the room, I picked my jaw up off the floor.

The class themselves were not really much of a problem. There was the odd one that called out something stupid and it's not as if I had time to learn their names, so they could.

The bell went and I dismissed them according to who was sat the most smartly and quietly. It took the annoying ones a lot longer to cotton on, it always does. They obviously enjoy being at school much more. Eventually, when there were only five of them left and I stopped dismissing anyone, they got the hint. The beauty of it is, it can all be done without actually broaching the subject, it's all in the actions and they seem to learn quicker that way.

Once all the children had gone, I began tidying up some of the desks, making myself useful in 'no man's land time,' the time when it is not acceptable to be seen to be leaving school but there is actually nothing for you to do. There was not a chance I was even picking up a pesky green pen or reading one word of those stories. The cheek of it!

After about ten minutes I'd tidied all the desks, put my coat on and packed my bag up, so I sat down to catch up on my social networking via my phone, waiting out the next ten minutes of 'no man's time.'

The head office lady popped her head around the door.

'Hello?' she said, looking me up and down, wondering what on earth I was doing.

'Hi,' I replied, smuggling my phone into my coat pocket and standing up, as if that would make me look busier.

'I've got Kaiser's mum at reception, he didn't come out and she's waiting for him.'

'Er ... okay. Let me go check the cloakroom.' I ran down to the cloakroom, no one. I called into the boys toilets. Nothing. I checked the neighbouring classrooms and the hall. Nobody. She was still there when I returned and she'd not done any searching herself.

'Well who did he go home with?'

'First of all, their teacher told me that they are just dismissed from class so I didn't see who he went with. Secondly, I have no idea who he is, I was in this class for ten minutes.'

'Oh, you'd know him if you saw him.' What kind of phrase was that? And EVERYBODY uses it!

'Well maybe I'd recognise him, but I wouldn't know it was Kaiser. He's probably gone home alone. Is he normally picked up by his mum?'

'Well not normally, no. He usually goes home on his own.' Once again I was stood there wondering why we were even bothering to have the conversation in the first place and why I was being led on a guilt trip again. There was one positive thing that occurred to me as she trailed back down the corridor. It was much nicer to see the back of her than the front and she'd suitably filled the remaining ten minutes of 'no man's time.' Off to the supermarket I went.

SATURDAY MORNING

In the faint distance I could hear that familiar tune. I stirred and rolled over. It continued, it wouldn't stop, why wouldn't it stop? I rolled over again and reached for the phone.

'Hello,' I grunted.

No answer.

'Hello,' I said, irritated, still half asleep.

No answer.

I peered at the screen as if through drunken goggles. It was my eight-thirty alarm that I'd set with my ringtone instead of my alarm noise by mistake.

WEDNESDAY MORNING

I'd woken up on time on this particular cloudy, Wednesday morning. I'd had my first cup of tea, been in the shower and done my hair and make-up. Then it got to that tricky dilemma that happens on so many mornings, what to wear? I'd not yet had a call and so was not sure of my plans for the day. I did my usual thing and changed into a clean pair of pyjamas so as not to dirty a casual or work outfit unnecessarily. There is always a problem with that though.

First of all, the postman views you as very lazy. Secondly, it looks strange, like perhaps you went to bed with your hair done and make-up on and managed to lie still in a suitable position all night just so you'd have less to do in the morning or maybe so you could get up later. And thirdly, if the postman believes point number two, he also gets the impression that you do not shower in a morning either. Luckily, my postman has not yet commented, but there is still time for that.

There's another issue as well. As I'm rather prudish, I'd never be seen dead outside in my pyjamas. This prevents me from doing any useful things outside until 8:45am when I officially know what I'm doing. (There are times though when I get an annoying call around 10am for an afternoon slot.) Anyway, this means I can't take anything out to the dryer (it's in the garage). I can't restock the cat's food or get any reserve supplies such as toilet rolls, shampoo, tins of beans, spaghetti, washing-up liquid, tinned tomatoes, deodorant, curry sauce, cleaning fluid, pasta shapes, washing powder or tuna (they're in the garage too). I also can't get any meals I made earlier out of the big freezer to defrost for teatime (you'll never guess, the big freezer's in the garage). I can't hang any washing out and I can't water the garden. It has occurred to me though that I obviously have an underlying feeling that someday soon, rationing may come back into force and before you ask, no, there is no car in our garage, and yes, you're right, it's probably because there is too much rubbish in there and it won't fit.

No sooner had I dressed myself in my pyjamas did the phone ring. This time it was definitely a phone call, not just my alarm.

'Hello.' After it got past eight o'clock and I'd had the time to contemplate a day without supply teaching, I always tried to make the 'hello' sound rather inconvenienced.

'Hi, is that Carly?' She was phoning my mobile, so I'm not sure who else she was expecting to answer.

'Speaking.'

'I've got a booking for you at St. Viktor's in Taxley.'

It wasn't a school I'd been to before and it was in the next town so I continued to make it difficult.

'Taxley? That's the next town over from me. I don't like to travel far, I just can't get back in time. How far is it?' Please be over ten miles, please be over ten miles I thought, one finger overlapping the other.

'The map is showing up that it's five miles from your house.'

Bummer. 'Right.'

'So can you do it then?'

'Yes, I suppose I can.'

'Are you sure?'

Was it wrong to try and think of an excuse at this late stage? It was. 'Yes,' I droned, 'I can do it.'

'Okay, it's a half day, they only need you for the morning.'

Notice how she told me that afterwards?! Little did she realise, I would have been much more likely to snap it up had she told me about the half-day beforehand. The thought of the afternoon off and a nice lunch at home made it very appealing.

I quickly charged upstairs, changed out of my pyjamas and found a suitable work outfit. It was another twenty minutes before I left the house armed with all my supplies like breakfast, snacks, bribes, and of course emergency lesson material.

I had an idea of the general area in which the school was in and the agency had text'd me the postcode. The satellite navigation was definitely trying to make me go the long way around and so I took my own shortcut, which of course turned out to be misguided. I was lost. I gave in to the satnav's instructions and approached from another direction, meaning I was really unsure where everything actually was.

'You have reached your destination,' she informed snottily. I knew I should have opted for the male voice.

I looked around, no school to be seen. Just down the road there were railings and a car park, I drove closer and glanced at the sign which said, 'St. Viktor's' and so I drove in.

The car park was rather empty and I was beginning to think that perhaps it was an overflow car park. I gathered all my things together and bustled out of the car.

Straight in front of me, attached to the large building, was a conservatory. I have to admit, I was rather confused. I could only imagine that this was part of the foundation unit for the three to five year olds. It was common for them to be housed in the new extensions. Besides, as awful as this sounds, the school was in a rather rundown area which meant that they would be blessed with much more money than the schools in the more affluent places so it was totally possible that they could have afforded a conservatory, perhaps it was even for the staff. I've previously worked in a new-build school that had a sun balcony just off the staffroom, on the south facing side of the building. It was a waste really, as the school also had a new-fangled timetable with a super early start and a twenty-five minute lunch, so we never had any time to use it.

I lugged my belongings around to the other side of the building as there was no entrance in sight. I passed the sign again which clearly stated, 'St. Viktor's, arrived at some double doors and went inside. There was a uniformed lady on reception, who was dressed in what looked rather like a beauticians outfit, all in white. The reception didn't seem to follow the same rules of layout for a typical school either. Even though they are all different, there are certain elements expected to be there, for example, a sign-in book that has the visitors badges integrated or a digital sign-in system. There is usually a school ethos pinned up on the wall and certificates mounted in frames to boast what awards the school has won. Nothing. It was also decorated in a very old fashioned way with pink, flowery wallpaper and I did think that this was rather odd, bearing in mind they could afford a conservatory. I concluded that this was their unique way of doing things, maybe to teach about history or perhaps it was to do with the religious element or the funding they got from the church.

'Can I help you?' asked the lady on reception with a thick, Essex accent which seemed to linger on the last syllable of every sentence.

'Carly Harley, supply.'

'You what, sorry?'

'I'm here on supply.'

'Are you here to visit someone because visitors don't usually come until ten o'clock, that's because we've to get everyone out of bed and do breakfast and things.'

Wait a sec ... it was all adding up in my head. 'Sorry, but where am I?'

'St. Viktor's.'

'St. Viktor's School?'

'Oh gosh, no. This is St. Viktor's Residential Home.'

I ran out of the building and got halfway to the car when I realised I'd left my coffee on the reception desk. Despite already being humiliated, I couldn't leave it behind. There was no way I was going to get through the rest of this so far disastrous day without it. It was also one of the expensive travel cups, dishwasher safe with a drinking hole that moved up and down instead of the cheap pound shop ones that slide and end up with a load of dried, rotten milk stuck under them! I was met by an applause and a cheer from the receptionist and what looked like the rest of her colleagues, now stood behind the reception desk, who had obviously just been told the hilarious tale of the lost supply teacher.

With a beetroot face I swiped the cup and exited backwards through the open double doors, turning only just in time to catch myself on the first step.

Back in the car I began driving around aimlessly trying to find the blasted school. I was going to have to make a call to the agency and admit the embarrassing event.

'Hello, Supply Teachers Direct, resourcing your school with quality teachers at low, low prices, Marie speaking, how may I help?' It wasn't a voice I was familiar with.

'Hi, it's Carly Harley.'

'Hi Carly, good to speak to you. How are you today?'

Why did they always do that? Make out that you had been friends for ages when you'd never even spoken to them before.

When you think about it, it's kind of freaky because they probably really do know who you are, looking at your picture every day on the computer file and perusing in detail your whole career history including how many times you went to the toilet last year. It's probably more worrying that they'd recognise you in the supermarket and smile, leaving you wondering who the heck they are, but then again, that actually happens a lot. But, seriously, when you apply to work with an agency, there can be no gaps in your CV, not even for a few weeks when you returned home from university. Everything has to be explained, just in case you were off doing something dodgy.

Every time you've not worked for a particular one for a few months, they phone you up, threatening to strike you off their list, as if it was your fault they'd not got you any work in the first place and wanting to know what you've been up to. Sometimes, they even insist on a new reference from a head teacher, even if you've only worked in schools for one day at a time and haven't even met the head!

'Er ... yeah, so I'm on my way to St. Viktor's.'

'You're not there yet?'

'No, I, er, ended up at an old people's home by mistake.'

'What?'

'Yes, well anyway, I'm still lost, my satnav says I'm here but I'm not.'

Marie then directed me to the school with the use of Google maps after I explained where I was. It turned out that the school was one side of the housing estate and the residential home was on the other. The school shared the same postcode as the estate. The tricky part was the one-way system which kept directing me away from the school and towards the residential home.

'I'll give the school a call and explain the situation,' said Marie.

'Thanks.'

I could clearly see the sign. I read it twice, 'St. Viktor's Primary School.'

I buzzed at the car park barrier.

'Hello.'

'Carly Harley, supply.'

The barrier lifted and I drove in. I circled the car park. No spaces.

I buzzed at the barrier again.

'Hello.'

'Carly Harley, supply. There are no spaces.'

The barrier lifted and I drove out.

All along the road were double yellow lines preventing me from parking my car. I took the first left turn down a side street, no spaces. I came back onto the road and took the second left turn down the second side street, none there either. This continued until I finally found a space on the fifth side street. It was now 8:45am. At least the school knew that I was in the vicinity.

I struggled out of the car with all my gear just as it started to bounce it down and raced towards the school gates. I must have looked a picture, rocketing head first like some kind of ostrich, my bag bouncing around, hitting my arm and then my leg like one of those wooden clacker toys.

I pressed the buzzer at the school gate, it was like déjà vu.

'Hello,' came the voice over the speaker.

'Carly Harley, supply.'

The gate buzzed and unlocked for a second and I pushed it open. I arrived at the main entrance and pressed yet another buzzer.

'Hello.'

'Carly Harley, supply. Buzzing yet again.'

The door unlocked for a second and I pushed it open.

'Yes, she's literally just walked through the door now,' said the lady behind the reception desk, a glass partition separating us. She had a sarcastic tone too.

'Sorry I'm late, I've had a nightmare morning...'

'Yes we've heard. An old people's home apparently. Well that's a step up from 'the dog ate my homework'.'

I honestly didn't know what to reply to that. Should I laugh? Was it a joke? If it was, it wasn't very funny, well, not at the time anyway. I smiled, well actually, no, I turned the corners of my mouth upwards ever so slightly and gave a blank stare.

'I'll show you to the classroom,' she said as she exited the office and I stood at yet another security door, waiting to be let in.

I could hear her chatting away. Being a member of the office staff means you have no concept of time. They're not bound by the strict time constraints that the rest of us in school are. If they fancy a twenty-minute break, they can have it, in fact two if they so wish and they can have it before the teaching staff or even after. I've noticed that many like to have it after, have full use of the staffroom for gossiping about colleagues while they're all in class with no danger of them walking in, plus, the longer you hold out until break time, the shorter the rest of the day is. There is an exception to the rule though, and that's when it's someone's birthday. Then they'll be the first in there, 'reserving' all the best cakes and taking them down to the office for their break time to make it 'fair'.

Eventually, she opened the door and let me through, I mean, it's not like I was and in a rush or anything. I still had my yoghurt to eat if I wanted to stay alive all morning and for all I knew, school could have already started.

It turned out that it hadn't started, it was your traditional nine o'clock start school and there were five minutes before the bell was to ring when I entered the room.

Concentrating on the important things first, I rummaged in my bag for that yoghurt I was telling you about and started shovelling in the biggest dollops I could with my teaspoon. Unfortunately, large dollops are too big for teaspoons and one of them landed on my top. I weighed the situation up. Which was more important before the children arrived in class, to have finished my yoghurt or to have a clean(ish) top? I went for the first and gobbled it all with three more shovelfuls, holding the yoghurt pot directly underneath my chin as I made my way over to the classroom sink.

I was glad they had one. It's quite essential to have a sink, especially one with drinking water after the government made a big thing about having water bottles for every child, and made teachers lives very difficult when it was insinuated that children should have a bottle of water on their table to squirt each other with or be able to get out of their seats to have a 'sip' whenever they didn't feel like doing any work.

Some of the new build schools have an 'art supplies' room and only one sink in there, with none in the classrooms. It was rather inconsiderate of them to do that really though because where are the supply teachers supposed to tip the dregs of their 'almost finished but now cold' coffees?

I gave my top a go with a blue paper towel with a bit of water on it. It wasn't doing much good so I rubbed a bit harder. I was left with a light coloured stain and blue bits of rolled up paper towel stuck to my top that just didn't want to come off.

I sighed loudly just as the bell rang and children started trailing in.

'Aww, not another supply teacher!' said one of the girls as she pulled out her chair.

I just loved welcomes like that. I wrote on the board 'Silent Reading' to buy myself some time.

It was then that I noticed the stack of feedback sheets on the teacher's desk, which was somewhat a mess. There were two alarming things. Firstly, there were more than twenty sheets and secondly, there were many types of handwriting, which could only mean one thing. Each one represented a different supply teacher. All of a sudden, I began to dread the day ahead.

There were about five students in the room at that point and they were reading quietly or in the process of getting a book so it wasn't too bad a start. Delve in, I thought, get to the heart of the problem.

'Where is your actual teacher?' I asked the girl who didn't want another supply teacher.

'She's poorly.'

'How long has she been poorly?'

'Ages!'

'Well how long is ages?'

'All year.'

'Really? All year?'

'It's not all year. It's been about six weeks,' the girl next to her chipped in.

'Six weeks. That's a long time. Any idea what's wrong with her?'

'Miss Cardle said that she had a poorly tummy. Maybe she's got a baby in it, she is quite fat.'

'Erm … I think you'd know if she was pregnant … well, if she was THAT pregnant!'

I came to my own conclusion; stress. A few more children arrived and so did the teaching assistant. She was very friendly.

'Hi, I'm Miss Cardle. Sorry I've only just come in now, I've been running the walking bus.'

'No worries, nice to meet you. I'm Mrs Harley.'

'Mrs? Wow! You don't look old enough to be married.'

Flattery! We were going to get on swimmingly!

'I'm old really, I'm twenty-eight.'

She didn't defend twenty-eight as being young, probably because she was much younger herself, perhaps working in school in the hopes of one day becoming a teacher. I could only hope the experience was suitably deterring her.

More and more children came in and I informed them about the silent reading.

'Miss, you've got something on your top,' called out one of the boys who had just sat himself down.

'Thank you for pointing that out to everyone. What's your name then?'

'Matty.'

I nodded at him to acknowledge that I'd heard and would be remembering his name.

Even though appearances can be deceiving, they actually do usually tell you a lot. It always amuses me how I can tell which are the sensible children. It was one of the sensible ones, who was wearing sensible shoes as opposed to trainers, that asked me if they could go to their reading partners. I looked to Miss Cardle for reassurance that this was something they normally did and she nodded. Two thirds of the class then exited, which felt like some kind of mass walk out, perhaps because they had yet another supply teacher. It was quite lonely without them and very quiet.

'How long does this reading partner thing last?' I asked Miss Cardle.

'About half an hour.'

This was a prime example of me asking the wrong question. I relished the thought of silent reading with ten children for another thirty minutes. Wonderful! I had not thought of anything to do with the children yet or had even taken the register, but I was feeling remarkably chilled out and with this set-up, who was bothered? No rush.

I wandered around the class, sipping coffee and having a good look around. Outside the classroom, in the playground, were some big wooden vegetable planters. It looked like carrots were being grown in one and onions in another. I also spotted some courgettes. They were in good condition too.

'Miss Cardle, I see you've got some vegetables growing out there. I've noticed lots of schools are trying to grow some of their own vegetables now.'

'Oh yes, it has been really successful. Our caretaker looks after it all and runs the clubs for the children to do their bit. Funny you should mention it, because he's not here today and I've been put in charge. He reckons next year he'll be able to make the school self-sophisticated. He's self-sophisticated himself you know.'

'Self-sophisticated?'

'You know, living off the land, just the posh words for it.'

'Do you mean self-sufficient?'

She screwed up her eyes and furrowed her brow in deep thought for a moment. 'Oh yeah, silly me,' she said with a giggle. 'I'm always saying things like that.' She looked down at her shoes in embarrassment and my eyes followed. Both had buckles. Both had bows. Both had a slight heel. They did not, however, look remotely similar, with one being black patent and one being a dull navy blue. I considered whether or not to say anything, bearing in mind that we were still in an awkward moment. I decided that I'd leave it for later, when her confidence had been built up again.

At that moment the reading partners returned. I

looked up at the clock in confusion. 9:15am, that couldn't be right, they weren't due back until at least 9:40am. Worst of all, they had people with them, little people.

I caught Miss Cardle's eye and she seemed quite alarmed at the fear on my face.

'Is everything okay, Mrs Harley? You look like you've seen a ghost.'

'Yes I'm fine, I'm just wondering what the little people are doing here.'

'You mean the reception children? They're the reading partners. Year four partner up with reception every morning.'

'Right, so they just partner up and we leave them to it?'

'Well, no. You have to teach them all first.'

'All fifty of them?! In this tiny classroom?'

'Well yes, but it's not that bad. Just get them all to sit down. The reception teacher will be here in a minute too to watch.'

'To watch? Not to deliver? Not to help?'

'Well I suppose she'll help if you ask her to, she just doesn't normally. It's because the teacher in here is the reading expert in school.'

'But she hasn't been here in six weeks. Have they just carried on with it anyway?'

'Actually, it's been nine and a half weeks and now you mention it, I suppose that is pretty weird that it's just continued.'

Perhaps this was the reason I'd seen so many feedback sheets on the desk with different handwriting, and the cause was not bad behaviour as I'd first assumed.

The children followed what I presumed to be their

usual routine with the year fours encouraging the four year olds to sit next to them on the carpet.

I smiled nervously at them. 'Good morning, children.'

'Good morning, Mrs …' at which point I heard each little person call me a different name such as, 'Williamson, Godber, Kingsley, Khan, Cowan and Roberts'. That must have been the succession of supply teachers effect. 'Harley. My name is Mrs Harley, children.'

'You've got the same name as that boy!' shouted a dark haired reception boy sat near the back. He was partnered with Matty.

'Is his name Mrs?' I joked, finding myself hilarious, as usual.

The little people gave me a confused stare. Of course, my humour was lost on them and I did my best to style it out, hoping Miss Cardle was too busy to notice. In fact, the least she could have done was laugh herself, but it was likely that it was over her head too.

'No. He is called Harley,' he said.

'Yes, that would be more the obvious choice.'

'He's not called obvious, I've just told you, he's called Harley.' At that point, a few of the brighter year fours laughed to save me from my downward spiral from sarcasm to the literal.

'Anyway, so that boy there is called Harley? Hello Harley.'

He was hunched over as he looked up, wary of the stranger that was me and gave a little wave but no vocals.

'Why are you called Harley? Harley is a boy's name!' asked one of the reception girls.

'Actually, it's a surname.' I thought better than that

and quickly reiterated, 'A last name, Harley was a last name first, then ...'

'Well it can't be because he is called Harley.'

'Anyway ...'

At that moment the reception teacher walked in, as if I'd been saved by the bell, or so I hoped.

The reception teacher made a bee-line for Miss Cardle. It was apparent that she was used to seeing a different teacher every time she entered the room. I was hoping to speak to her before commencing but they just chatted quietly amongst themselves whilst glancing over, making it more than obvious that their subject of conversation was me. I was now certain that the large stack of feedback sheets was definitely due to this and not down to the behaviour of the children. Don't get me wrong, they weren't perfect, but up to this point, they'd been pretty good.

The reception children couldn't sit still for very long, so while they were having their chin wag, I pulled something out of the air.

'Who can tell me what they did yesterday?' If you thought the bouncy voice was annoying, we're now in super bouncy mode, just in an attempt to get the little children to actually look at you.

There were plenty of the year fours with their hands up. Hmm ... not exactly what I was looking for.

'I'll tell you what. Reception children, turn and face your reading partner and find out from them what they did yesterday.'

'I can't remember, Miss,' said Matty. What a surprise!

'Well, ask a year four nearby then.' It annoyed me that he'd won. We both knew that I didn't want to give him the opportunity to chat to any of his mates, but it was easier to let him do that than it was for me to try to give him information I didn't know but that he should have known. It wasn't worth the energy.

I took a moment to take a swig from the travel cup.

'Okay, reception children,' I began.

'It's Green Class,' called the reception class' teacher from across the room. She could tell me that and criticise, but nothing else?

'Green Class, who can tell me what their reading partner did yesterday?'

There were a few hands. I chose one of the boys near the front.

He gave a blank stare and recoiled from me.

'Can you remember what your partner did yesterday?' I asked softly.

He continued to stare and then looked at his partner, trying to telepathically receive the information.

I gave his partner 'the eye' and the direction motion with my head.

She whispered into his ear.

'Smash,' he said, relieved.

I looked at his partner, puzzled.

'Maths, Miss,' she said, shaking her head.

I concluded it was time to move on. I looked in the direction of Miss Cardle and the other teacher in attempt to get some assistance, but conveniently, despite glancing over frequently, when I needed them, they refrained from staring.

I racked my brains. Phonics. That's what the little people do. Fortunately, I'd had some training on phonics in one of the schools I was in but never rarely had the cause to use it. I had no resources and no sound cards so I just wrote them up on the board, hoping that, even if the little ones didn't know them, the year fours would make it sound like they did. All went smoothly for the subsequent four minutes until I ran out of the simple sounds and daren't venture onto the more tricky ones.

Now the thought did enter my head, 'reading partners' and perhaps I should try to fall in with that somehow. I had the most ingenious idea, although I'm sure that it's not what they meant when they came up with the term, 'reading partners'.

'For the last fifteen minutes, Green Class are going to quickly choose a book that they'd like their reading partner to read to them.'

'Aww, Miss! We always do this!' It seemed that the brilliant idea was not only mine.

They all got up and went off in search of exciting books and I went over to Miss Cardle and the other teacher to find out what was so important that they could not offer me any help whatsoever.

'See you found the golden ticket then?' said reception's teacher.

'Excuse me?' I had no idea what she was going on about.

'We usually see how long it takes the supply teacher to think of that activity. You were pretty quick as it happens.'

'I see,' I replied, shocked that I'd been part of some weird experiment.

As you can imagine, I wasn't very impressed with their inside joke at my expense. It turned out that this teacher was a NQT, which did surprise me as quite often they are not quite so sure of themselves and are also eager to please fellow and more experienced teachers and prepared do most you ask them to, even when they're unreasonable. Of course it all changes the following year, when they realise that their year group partner has hardly done anything while they've been working like a donkey producing reams of planning, super in-depth marking that the children never read and interactive whiteboard presentations that are so detailed that any teacher could teach from them without even looking at the planning. That's when they scale back and start doing half of the work for the two of them instead of all of it. At least it cuts their hundred hour week down to a more manageable seventy. A few years down the line, the cycle has come full circle and they've got their very own NQT year group partner.

So the 'reading stories to the little ones' was going well. There was only one pair still looking for a book. Matty and his partner.

'Matty,' I called to get his attention whilst selecting a picture book from a nearby shelf. 'Sit down,' and I passed him the book. The two did so and at least looked occupied with the book until I gave the next instruction, sometime later.

Meanwhile, I took the opportunity to quiz the NQT teacher.

'So, did you do a PGCE then or a teaching degree?' I asked.

'Oh, a teaching degree, of course. PGCE's produce rubbish teachers.' Strike one. Yes, I did a PGCE.

'Oh, I see. Does that mean all secondary teachers bar ones that specialise in physical education are rubbish then?'

'Erm ... it's different for them.'

'Oh right. Must be easier to teach in secondary then.' Definitely NOT! I can vouch for that. They both have their own difficulties.

'How's your job hunt going then? Have you been

for many interviews?' she asked.

'Pardon?'

'Some people just aren't good at the interviews are they? Or is it the lesson you find hard? It is hard for some people to be put on the spot. I didn't think you did too badly today though. I do think that you could be a little more relaxed with the behaviour mind ... encourage the children to talk more and be active ... get them jumping up and down and walking around the room.' I had to pinch myself to check I was hearing this. I wondered how to respond.

'I'm sorry ... did you think I was an NQT?'

'Well no, not yet obviously, you've got to get a teaching post first.'

'I'm flattered that you think I'm so young! What a compliment!' I then addressed the class, 'Right, Green Class, line up by the door please.'

'Wait, they've got another ten minutes yet,' she stammered.

'I'm giving them something active to do ... walking back to class,' I grinned.

I flicked through one of my differentiated Maths books, a scared resource for supply teachers, and found some work on measuring with a rule (apparently they'd been working on it recently). It was doable for supply, not too complex, and something they actually needed to know. I gave the book to Miss Cardle in the hope that she'd actually be allowed to do the photocopying.

Whilst she was out of the room I asked the children to get into their Maths groups. I was soon willing her to return speedily as Matty was insisting that he was in Hexagon group and Fiona was adamant that he was not. Deliel did his best to persuade me that he had been moved last lesson to have a permanent place next to him on what looked like a 'naughty table', standing alone at the front of the room, with unsurprisingly, only one chair parked behind it.

'Ok guys, I can see that this is obviously causing a problem, so Matty, you'll have to sit next to Sarah.' She was the only person who has a space next to her.

The whole class gasped and held their breath in disbelief and Matty stared at me, a plead in his eyes. The penny dropped. There was a reason Sarah had no-one sat next to her, it was because no-one wanted to. I hated the fact that I'd drawn attention to it now, I felt like I'd initiated an attack against the poor girl. I was about to stand my ground and still make him sit there, I suppose in some ways as a kind of 'apology' to her, but I did worry it could make things spiral. Perhaps he'd refuse or call her nasty things, all of which I would gladly avoid. At that moment he said the most sensible thing and saved himself, Sarah and me from the uncomfortable atmosphere.

'Actually, Miss,' he said, guiltily. 'I sit on square table. I'll just go sit there.'

I was comfortable with that compromise, despite the slight defiance.

'Okay, year four,' I began. 'We're going to be looking at measuring today.' I held up a rule. 'What is this?' I asked.

It was my own fault for the shouting out that followed as I'd forgotten to insert words from the supply teachers pre-emptive dictionary which clearly states that every question should start with, 'Don't shout out, put your hand up, what/why/when...,' you catch my drift.

Amidst the loud din I picked out the word 'ruler' many times. So that was what they called it and that was that.

'Put your hand up if you've done this before.' The show of five hands out of the full class prompted my next move. 'Deliel is now going to hand out the rulers so we can all have a good look at them.' The only rulers in the classroom were the fifteen centimetre long ones (short rulers) with centimetres on one side and inches on the other.

There is a reason that some teachers keep rulers locked up in a drawer or cupboard somewhere, sacrificing the children's need to practise using one, even for simple underlining tasks and I predicted the reason was exactly the same in this classroom as the many others with a lack of present rulers. Only five rulers had been handed out when one hurtled across the room. The child hadn't thrown it though, of course, he'd just got a little over enthusiastic with his new 'lightsaber'. I was just about to do my ten to one countdown, a favourite of mine, when there was an overwhelming shrill ringing loudly throughout the building. Oh great! A fire alarm!

'Right children, can you please...'

'Miss, it's a test,' yelled Matty over the noise.

'In the middle of the day?' I questioned.

'Yeah, it happens every week.'

Sure enough, a few seconds later the noise stopped. I continued hesitantly and slightly flustered with the interruption mid-flow, 'Okay, so as I said before, we are going to be learning about measuring. Can everyone please hold up their ruler.' I did contemplate explaining its real name, 'a rule', but I didn't want to confuse them any further ... another lesson for another teacher.

The children did so eagerly.

'Let me re-phrase that. Hold up your ruler and keep it still please. In other words, Matty, without swinging it near another person's head.'

I waited, about ninety seconds in total, until everyone was completely still. It felt like forever.

'Let's look at the numbers on our measuring instrument. What can you tell me about them?'

Isabel, the sensibly dressed one, responded with a raised hand, 'The numbers go up in order,' she said.

'Yes, they certainly do,' I replied, surprised that she hadn't thought of anything more sophisticated. 'Can you think of anything else?'

'They've got lines in between them?'

'Also true. What about the numbers on the other side?'

Matty had his hand up, a pleasant surprise.

I nodded at him to respond.

'The gaps between the numbers are bigger on one side.'

'Brilliant! Can we all have a really good look at our rulers and find the side where the numbers are further apart?'

Now, I know that all the non-teachers out there are going to be thinking, what on earth is she doing, dragging all this out and all, but honestly, the teachers will vouch for this, every eventuality must be covered if you want them to get the right answer in the end because they will go with their first thought in any situation. You have to work out all the mistakes they could possibly make before they make them and tell them not to do it. It's a complete nightmare!

At that moment, noise could be heard on the corridor and Isabel had her arm stretched in the air so enthusiastically I thought she might pull a muscle.

'Yes, Isabel?' I said eagerly.

'Miss, it's time for Maths.'

I replied in confusion, 'Yes, that's what we're doing now, Maths.'

'I know, but real Maths.'

I was annoyed at that comment and was just about to take it the way it sounded when the door opened, Miss Cardle bustled in with some very large sheets of paper and the text book I'd given her, followed by a steady flow of children from other classes.

'Can we go then, Miss?' asked Isabel.

'Do you all move around for Maths then?'

'Yes.'

'Okay, year four, can you make sure your tables are tidy and then go to your Maths class please.' At least ninety per cent of them left. The other children took their places at the tables and these children were remarkably smaller than the others.

'What year are you in?' I asked one of the boys.

'Year three,' he replied. Year three was okay.

'And what year are you in?' I asked the boy sat next to him.

'Year two,' he said, shyly.

Oh great. INFANTS! So it turned out that this class was mostly year twos working at expected levels and some year three children working below average. I'd had some photocopying done for a year four class, and yes, it was differentiated, but the lowest level of work on the sheet was aimed at average year threes. This day was just getting better and better!

Now, as I was only doing the morning, I was aware of the need to not overdo it on work that needed marking as that was a lunchtime I'd have to stay marking whilst not getting paid. I had planned for the measuring work to be done in books but at this point, I decided to go for paper that could be carefully filed at the end of the lesson in the recycling bin. With what I was about to find out next, I was glad that I'd already made that decision.

Miss Cardle was sat at another teachers desk at the back of the room, one which I assumed must have belonged to her. She was going through some paperwork.

'Have you got those photocopies for me please, Miss Cardle?'

'Oh yes, here they are,' she said, handing me sheets of A3 paper along with my text book.

'Miss Cardle, you've blown them up to A3,' I said, confused.

'Oh yes, well there wasn't any A4 paper left so I did them on A3 instead.'

'Why not just copy them at the normal size on A3 then?'

'Well, I didn't want to waste the paper. I thought it would be a good idea so they could see the questions better.'

'But we are doing measuring. The measurements in the book are precise. The lower ability work only had lines on it that measured in whole centimetres.' I reached for a rule from a neighbouring table and measured the first line on the lower ability section. 'This line now measures 14.6cm. It is also the shortest line and these rulers only go up to 15cm.'

She gave me an embarrassed look, in fact, I thought she may burst into tears and then I worried about the consequences of that.

'Never mind,' I said, reassuringly. 'I'll just think of something else to do.'

'I ... I just have to go and do some things in the vegetable garden,' she announced. 'The caretaker said I have to tickle the courgettes.'

'I see,' I agreed. 'Pollinating season.' It was something I was used to doing myself on my own vegetable patch.

She nodded and I concluded that she needed a few moments out anyway.

Before leaving the classroom, she collected some gardening tools such as a trowel, a fork and gloves, yet no paintbrush to do the pollinating with. I assumed at that point that she'd forgotten it and would be back or perhaps she'd left it outside.

I returned my attention to the class as she left. 'Okay children, on your whiteboards, see if you can write out the two times table and the five times tables as quickly as you can.'

They had quite a good work ethic and carried out my instructions eagerly. A few of them finished earlier than the others and I employed the KBB technique that I'm sure so many teachers will be familiar with (Keep the Brats Busy) by asking them to wipe it off and write it backwards.

Miss Cardle was now outside our classroom window, tending to the courgettes. From a distance, whatever she was doing looked very strange, so I edged closer. Not close enough to make her feel stared at, but close enough to get a better look. I stood there in amazement, watching her touch the courgettes in a weird way as I took another swig of my now, cold coffee. All I can say is, it's a good job that I was standing next to the sink as the moment I swigged was the moment the penny dropped and I realised that she was 'tickling the courgettes' LITERALLY. Coffee was sprayed all over the sink, all over the taps and all over the window.

I reached for a paper towel from the holder next to the sink. None. Another consequence of the 'real' teacher being off.

'Can someone fetch me some toilet roll please?'

Ten children stood up at once and headed for the door.

'Yes, we'll just have one doing that job thank you,' and I pointed to the boy who was nearest the door which gave the impression my selection process was survival of the fittest.

I placed my cup next to the computer at the front of the room, it was cold anyway.

'Is that coffee, Miss?' asked one of the boys, sat near the front.

'Yes, it is. I need it to keep me going.'

'Do you like coffee, Miss?'

'As it happens I do, you'd never believe it would you? I prefer tea, but it doesn't taste as nice in those cups ...' I realised I was letting myself get drawn in to a 'If we get Miss to talk about herself, we won't have to do any work' conversations. It was nice how the younger ones were interested in you as a person though, rather than you as a teacher, even if the relentless questions about how many kids you had and how old you were got a bit wearing at times.

The 'fittest' boy rushed back with the paper towels and I wiped down the window and the sink.

'Miss, you've got something on your top,' said the same boy who'd asked about the coffee. Trust him to notice. He seemed quite pleased with his own observation skills.

'Yes, I know that,' I replied, a frustrated tone in my

voice. 'Rub off your whiteboards now please, chil...'

I was interrupted by the shrill again. Surely they didn't have two scheduled tests during in school time. We waited a few moments but the noise continued. Then we heard tables and chairs moving in the class next door and took that as our cue. I had no idea where we'd be lining up. It was a case of 'follow the teaching assistant' in situations like this, but she was still outside 'tickling' her courgettes.

'Let's sensibly make our way outside please, making sure we walk, do not talk and stay in a line.' There was no other adult and so I was the last one out of the classroom, rather than lead them, to make sure all in my care had vacated the room, my laminated register in tow. I followed the children, who executed the operation rather smoothly, I might add, through swinging doors, along corridors, down steps and yet more doors. It did seem rather a long trek to the fire assembly point.

Once outside, the children split to get into the lines of their respective classes. I scanned the lines to try and find a line of children that I vaguely recognised. It was Miss Cardle I spotted first. I hurried over. I was pleased that she had taken the initiative and organised the year four children accordingly. They were all lined up smartly in front of her and I stood with them, waiting to be addressed by someone important, such as the head or deputy head.

We ran through the register while we waited and thankfully, everyone was present. There were some worried faces on the people who I assumed were the 'important' people and they were chatting anxiously amongst themselves and then speaking to others who shook their heads at them, seemingly clueless. One of them dashed back into the building while the other took hold of the gramophone.

'It appears that class 4D are missing. Mr Fenwick is currently dealing with the situation so we need you all to wait quietly.'

Oh dear, a missing class! Hang on a minute, my class was called 4D wasn't it?

'Miss Cardle, isn't that our class?' I whispered, so as not to draw attention to ourselves.

'What?'

'Is our class 4D?'

'Yes.'

'Did you not just hear what that guy said?'

'No, I was tying a shoelace.'

'Well, someone has just gone in to look for us. You best dash over there and tell them we're here!'

She hesitated and then walked over to the man with the gramophone. Yes, she walked, with no sense of urgency at all. He threw his hands in the air in reaction to whatever she'd said, almost forgetting he was holding the gramophone as he swung it above his head and almost dropped it and then he charged over to me and I began to panic.

'This class is NOT supposed to line up here,' he barked.

'Er ... yes, I'm sorry about that, I didn't realise ...'

At that moment, the fire brigade emerged from the building and I wanted the ground to swallow me whole.

The gramophone man got distracted and raced over to them, probably to tell them not to look for the missing kids.

A few minutes later, he made another announcement.

'I am very disappointed,' he said. Was he going to

shame me in front of the whole school? 'Someone here has done a very, very silly thing. This was not a planned fire drill. The fire brigade have confirmed that the alarm went off because one of you thought it would be funny to press the button. So that means that someone who really needs their help is not getting the help of the fire fighters now because of someone at our school being so selfish. If I find out who that person is they will lose the rest of their play times and dinner times until the holidays! If it happens again and the fire brigade have to come out again then the school will be charged a lot of money and I will happily give the bill to the parents of the child that did it.'

There was a stony silence and I was relieved that the fire brigade had not turned up on my account but because it had been flagged up as a real fire.

The classes were dismissed, row by row, and the man who'd dashed inside to rescue us all returned. It turned out he was the head teacher. He waited until all the classes had gone before he said his piece.

'I am very disappointed 4D,' he began. 'Miss ...' and he looked at me for my name.

'Harley.'

'Miss Harley is a visitor in this school and cannot be expected to know exactly where you line up in a fire drill. You, however, practised this last week and should know where you are supposed to line up. It is your job to help Miss Harley when she is in school. If today we had had a real fire, I would have been looking for you and putting myself in very serious danger. Go and line up in the place 4D should line up when we have a fire drill.'

They moved, silently and stealthily to the other side of the playground and lined up. At least I knew where it was now, not that it would matter now anyway, it was useless information, a case of too little, too late.

The head teacher left us and I had my own bit to say. 'I have to say, year four, I'm somewhat embarrassed. The mistake that was made today could have had serious consequences and although it may not seem like a big deal because nothing bad happened, it could have been very different. I do expect your behaviour for the rest of the day to show that you are thinking seriously about how to improve.' Here's a handy hint that I employed there: always guilt trip where you can for an easier life. Another good idea is to instantly raise your standards ten times over after such a 'talking to'. 'Right children, I expect you to walk back to class in absolute silence. Off you go.'

I led the front of the line, taking three steps walking forwards and then about six walking backwards in a repeating pattern to scan over the faces with my 'stern scowl'. Every time I heard the slightest murmur, I turned around and stopped the line from moving forwards. I was going all out for Victorian style behaviour. Bring it back, that's what I say! We arrived at the door to get into the building and I'm sure you'll be really surprised to find out that it was locked and that Miss Cardle did not have a fob. I sent her out of the school gate and around to the office via the pavement. I mean, surely that's not right … and so many are like that. The building cannot be entered unless you have a key, fob or code, but the playground can be entered as the gates are left unlocked, so if a child really wanted to escape, they could, because there is no problem with leaving the building, you just push a big green button and the doors release.

It was quite hard keeping up the stern bravado for the lengthy amount of time it took Miss Cardle to walk around to the office, make her way through school and get to the other side of our locked door.

We made our way through the corridors and up the stairs. Just as we were about to go through the set of double doors near a classroom, a booming voice could be heard. It was the teacher from the classroom next door bawling out the year twos and threes from the Maths class I'd been teaching. Instead of lining up quietly, waiting for us to return, the children had taken to rolling around on the carpet and performing other 'James Bond' style actions such as sliding along the corridor on their knees and attempting to do really bad handstands. It appeared this was another thing I was now responsible for, being in two places at once.

I guess it's just the nature of supply and I've accepted that that's just the way it is. I'm never fully in the know and people always forget to tell me things that may be important or that I might need to know, such as, that the class would be waiting for me. I always find out that I've done something wrong after it's happened, so technically, it's not actually doing anything wrong. It goes the other way too though. Sometimes, I'll be bombarded with useless information that I certainly do not need or care to know for one day teaching on supply.

I sent 4D off to their Maths classes for the second time and had the Maths class I was now teaching apologise to the teacher next door before returning to their seats in an attempt to start again.

'How many minutes until break time, Miss Cardle?' I questioned.

'Three minutes.'

'Let's see who's sitting really sensibly,' I said, with manipulation all over it. 'I'm looking for someone to come and be the teacher at the front for the game 'hangman'.'

The tallest arms, the tightest lips, the most folded arms and the deepest held breaths instantly came into play. I chose one that hadn't tried so hard and the sound of the half groan, half sigh from the rest of them filled the room.

A few minutes later and we were saved by the bell. Hopefully, with a new start after playtime, we'd be able to salvage the rest of the morning.

As the children exited I took the opportunity to pull a snack from my bag and see if the outside world deemed me popular. Indeed, they did. Ten missed calls. Alarm bells started to ring with that many. All the calls were from one of the agencies I work with regularly. I also had a text message which read, 'Hi Carly, Belle Cowston Juniors are wondering where you are. Is everything okay?'

The sinking feeling dropped like a tonne of bricks from my gullet, right through the floor. Was I supposed to be at another school? I quickly checked the diary on my phone but there was nothing scheduled, but now it had been mentioned, I vaguely remembered booking it in. I scoured through the other days frantically to discover that I'd logged the booking in August, the only month I couldn't possibly be needed! It was a nice school, close to my house and I went there often. I could kiss goodbye to that relationship.

I phoned the agency in a panic. 'Hello, yes, Carly Harley here, have you sorted it? I'm at another school, I'm so sorry, I didn't realise.' All the words spilled from my mouth giving no time for the agent to respond.

'It's fine. We've sorted it. The school were just concerned that something terrible might have happened.'

The agent seemed fine about it, but I wasn't sure. I'd caused grief again, of course, without realising. I was worked up for the rest of the day then. Feeling as guilty as could be after taking a booking from another agency and not showing up to the one I'd previously booked.

I slumped in the chair and rubbed my face with my hands, attempting to de-tense the muscles. It was then that the teacher from next door waltzed in. I prepared myself for yet another telling off.

'With all the disruption regarding the shed load of supply teachers, I've been asked to provide planning for all the Literacy lessons for continued learning,' she informed. 'Today is a really simple lesson, we are looking at the book, 'Goodnight Mr Tom' and all you have to do is watch the film.'

'Oh that's brilliant, thanks. Have you got the DVD then?'

'I'm afraid we only have it on video. Don't worry though, we watched it yesterday, so I'll send some children round with it in the first ten minutes of the lesson.'

'That's brilliant, thanks.' At least it would only mean plugging the video player into the wall for the projector. Sounded like a nice, easy lesson and I loved that film too.

I made the effort to make the long journey downstairs to collect the children to find that they were not there and Miss Cardle had collected them for me and had taken them up the other way. I dashed back up the stairs to avoid a situation like the one that had occurred before playtime, like, children with no teacher.

I wasn't sure I could leave Miss Cardle with them in complete confidence after the shenanigans that had unfolded thus far.

I made it, flustered, tearing at my coat as I sweated, watching the children approach behind Miss Cardle. I continued the Victorian style behaviour approach and marched up and down the corridor inspecting and commenting on everything about them such as shirts not tucked in, trousers too low or tucked into socks, hands in pockets, slight mutterings, slouched shoulders and those stood on slight diagonals instead of facing straight forward. I actually enjoy being a hard task master. It gives me great satisfaction when they pander to my every whim.

We marched purposefully into the classroom and took our seats.

'Despite a difficult morning, 4D has a lovely treat in store for our Literacy lesson. We are going to be watching the film, 'Goodnight Mr Tom'.'

Fists clenched all around the room and 'yes's' hissed through many a set of gritted teeth, but happy gritted teeth.

'However,' I continued, 'there is tidying up that needs to be done first.'

They all began scrambling to get hold of the same things to put away like rulers and pencil pots.

'I'm still waiting 4D,' I whispered, in an attempt to win back their attention. 'Don't do anything yet,' I said quietly, and these are the crucial words that must be said before any instructions are given out. Some teachers phrase it differently like, 'don't do anything until I say go' but either way, it's back to that pre-emptive attitude that has to know how they will react before they do to prevent anarchy in every mundane and seemingly simple task.

I continued to whisper, so they had to listen carefully. I suppose, tapping into our natural urge to want to eavesdrop on a conversation we shouldn't be listening to, just as the noisiest class suddenly goes silent once two teachers begin chatting to one another quietly in the presence of the class. They don't want to feel like they're missing anything. 'Make sure everything is off the floor, don't do it yet, I can see people twitching, all books need to be in neat piles, and equipment organisers should be tidy, still listening children, I haven't finished. Rulers need to be collected and then you need to be sat smartly at your tables.' I paused, enjoying their suspense. 'Go!'

The rush ensued of busy children shuffling around. Most didn't need to be out of their seats but that didn't mean that they weren't. I wandered around, giving the usual type of boys who thought this was their extra playtime as tidying was women's work, specific jobs to do, usually picking rubbish up from the floor as a subtle punishment for thinking they were so self-important.

Within minutes the place was looking much better and everyone was sitting smartly, hoping to impress and eradicate the impressions made earlier.

The door opened and I expected it to be the children from next with the video and the video player but it was another member of staff. I looked over to see if I could help but she avoided eye contact with me and asked the child nearest the door, 'Who is that?'

'Another supply teacher,' was the reply.

The woman shrugged and then exited with no acknowledgement to me at all.

We waited for a few moments. I'd hoped by now that the video would have arrived. The children were definitely trying their best to behave exceptionally, so much so that, every time there was a muttering sound, one girl took it upon her to shush everyone and then the others did the same which just turned into one big shush competition.

'Look children, I do appreciate that there are pupils here who are trying to help me out by making sure that everyone stays quiet, but the good news for you is that I actually get paid for this job you know, that's right, I don't do it for free or for the fun of it, so you don't need to worry about trying to do my job. Have a rest today and let me have a go.'

That stunned a few of them, probably because they'd found out that I didn't do the job for fun.

'Miss,' said Matty.

'Yes ...' I couldn't believe we were still waiting.

'You've got something on your top.'

'Thank you for pointing that out to everyone. I spilt something earlier and I can't get it out.'

'At least you're not wearing odd shoes though,' he continued loudly, 'like Miss Cardle.'

He had assumed that she was out of the class on an errand as she was out of his sight, therefore, out of his mind, but she was, however, sat at the back of the room at her desk.

'What was that?' she called. 'Did I hear my name?'

'Oh, it was nothing, Miss Cardle,' I said reassuringly. 'You must have heard us wrong.' I gave Matty 'the glare'. Matty understood 'the glare' and said no more.

Jamie though, sat next to him, did not understand 'the glare'. 'He did say Miss Cardle's name. He was telling everyone how she's wearing odd shoes AGAIN. It happens all the time.'

This time she heard and to top it off, the heads of the whole class swivelled in one go and looked under the desk to her shoes, clearly odd, as she crossed one foot in front of the other and dragged them into herself, in an attempt to disguise the reality.

The atmosphere was broken by a knock at the door and the gentle creak of it opening. It was the children from next door, what a relief. There were three of them. One to open the door and two to manoeuvre the beast. The contraption was not as I'd imagined. It was emerging from the Jurassic Park era or at least my own school days. Tables, chairs and children had to be moved to wheel in the almighty stand with the rather small, fifteen inch, replacement video/TV in the original's place.

'Is this what your class watched 'Goodnight Mr Tom' on?' I asked.

'Yeah,' they replied, sounding if it was even more hard work than I was just imagining.

Once positioned at the front, they left the room. I decided it would be best to get the children as close to the television as possible. We moved chairs and tables until we ended up with half of the children sat on tables just inches away from it and tables behind, the rest of the class sat on them.

It was then, I realised, yes, I should have checked earlier, but in the heat of the moment, I didn't, that the lead to plug the TV in was really short and would not reach the plug socket on the wall. I moved the giant stand closer, backward and left, up to the wall. It still wouldn't reach as the computer desk was in the way. Extension was a dirty word and probably wouldn't be PAT tested so there was no point going in search for one of those.

We moved the chairs and tables again and trundled the giant over to the other side of the room where there was much less furniture. There was a single socket there that television plug could just about reach but the socket was in use. Class 4D's fish tank filter was using said socket, but I concluded that the fish would survive filter-less until lunch time.

By the measure of the day so far, I was pleasantly surprised when the TV turned on without any drama. Remote studying, consecutive button pressing and children who thought they knew much better ensued for a few moments and then of course there was the rewinding that needed to be carried out as next door hadn't bothered to do that. But could you blame them, as there was only the teacher old enough to realise that that's what had to be done and it had probably been so long since she'd done it she'd forgotten.

I turned the lights out, waited for everyone to be silent and still and then pressed play. This would have been a great opportunity for getting some marking done, but as it turned out, I didn't have any. I'd still have to stay at school for at least ten minutes before leaving though, even though it would be lunch time. I'm rather aware of what leaving straight after the bell makes you look like.

Before I settled down to watch it with them, I paced around the room to encourage the quietness that we had worked so hard on.

'Miss ...' came that oh so annoying whine. 'Miss, his elbow is digging into me.'

'Right, okay, can you move down here then please,' I said, irritated and pointing to a nearby chair.

'Miss, can I move?' asked Matty.

'No, I'm not having everyone moving.'

He scowled at me in reply and I pretended I hadn't seen him to avoid having to deal with it, choosing my battles carefully.

I strolled around the back of the tight huddle to the other side of the class, doing 'the behaviour rounds', but quickly made my way back. Someone had dropped one, and it really did stink!

'Miss, it smells, someone's farted,' shouted Jamie.

'Eugh Jamie, it 'were you!' screamed the girl sat next to him, disgusted.

'No it wasn't, Miss!' he protested.

I made the quick decision to remove him from the situation, otherwise we'd be discussing this all lesson. 'Jamie, I wondered if you could do me a favour and see if you can get some paper towels for our classroom?'

He was happy to help and jumped at the prospect of being trusted with an 'important' errand.

We continued watching, despite some of the children already showing signs of restlessness. I have to admit, it annoyed me somewhat. I'm a massive fan of historical dramas. There is so much to be learnt from the characters and the setting, especially when the story affects the emotions. It was like going to the cinema on a Saturday afternoon and having the experience destroyed by all the annoying kids.

Suddenly, the noisy bell began again, wailing on and on. Not again. I reached over to the TV and flicked the switch.

'Right 4D, we know how to do it, in silence and you KNOW where to line up.'

As we left the classroom, Jamie returned with the paper towels and a frightened look in his eye. I'd not anticipated that repeated fire drills were so scary, although, perhaps it was a real fire this time. I threw them in the room and we both joined the back of our line.

Outside in the playground 4D lined up sensibly in the correct place and the head teacher sported us a patronising thumbs up from across the way, which I could only roll my eyes at.

We waited and waited and waited ... until the fire brigade turned up, yet again. What a coincidence to have a false alarm and a real fire in one day. Although it turned out it wasn't a real fire and once again, the button had been pressed by a prankster for the second time that morning.

This time, however, the culprit had not been so smart and had done the deed near the school office, where a member of the office staff had seen him do it.

The deputy head stood in front of us with his gramophone again. 'Jamie Ramsbottom,' he bellowed.

The whole school began looking around and muttering. It certainly sounded like this boy was in trouble, well, that's if it was a boy because Jamie is a girls' name too these days.

'Jamie Ramsbottom, get yourself in front of me this second!'

There was pushing and shoving and some kind of kafuffle in 4D's line. Jamie started walking forward, sheepishly. Of all the possible Jamie's in the entire school! I knew at that moment what had happened. He stood there, in the middle of the playground, head down, shoulders over, refusing to make eye contact with anyone.

The entire school was dismissed again, bar 4D. At least this time I was actually supposed to be teaching this class. I was called over to participate in the 'chat' for Jamie, the deputy head and now the headmaster were having.

'We know it was you, Jamie, so there is no point in denying it,' insisted the deputy head.

Jamie just started bawling. It was quite hard to make out what he was saying through the sobs and short, sharp breaths. 'But I only did it that time. I didn't do it before. I just wanted everyone to go outside so they'd stop saying that I farted and stop picking on me.'

'And what were you actually doing out of the classroom?'

'Getting some paper towels for Miss.'

Both adults gave me 'the look', but without all the information, and I was obviously going to be unable to give my reasoning, and why should they not assume that I'd allowed him to play me like a fiddle? Every decision carried its own risk. Unfortunately, being on supply did not give you access to the full set of knowledge before having to employ a decision. That's just the way it was.

The carted Jamie off to make some kind of example of him and sent me back on the third journey from the playground to the classroom. We took it slow, there was no point in this day any longer.

Back in class I clock-watched for the remaining twenty minutes until the bell went for lunch time. It would certainly be a day that I wouldn't forget. I planned my shopping list on a piece of scrap paper as it was my intention to call in at the supermarket near my house on the way home.

After what seemed like a lifetime the bell finally went and I sent them to lunch. Usually, I'd do this table by table but it was quicker to get rid of them all at once. I didn't even ask them to put the chairs and tables back, I thought it'd be easier to do it myself once they'd gone.

Plus, I'd have to kill at least ten minutes after the morning had officially finished.

I unplugged the TV and wheeled the stand next door, returned all the chairs and tables to their previous homes and plugged the filter for the fish tank back in. I felt quite proud of myself for remembering to do that. There was a problem though, it didn't appear to be working. There was a switch on the side with different settings. I flicked it onto the top setting. Suddenly, the water began whirling around rapidly, taking the poor fish with it, their tails pointing upwards, as if they were being swept down the drain. I panicked and tried to change the setting but none of them worked, it seemed to be stuck on the strongest. I kept flicking the switch frantically. Nothing.

Eventually, I turned the filter back off at that plug and the whirling stopped. Three little fishes (there were only three in the tank) floated gracefully to the top and turned upside down.

Like a robber, I crept over to my bag, collected all my belongings and exited the room as quickly as I could. I dashed through the dining room, worried I'd be stopped and questioned about the deaths before I'd made my escape.

Standing there like a bouncer, blocking the only exit in the dining room which led to the office, was a nursery child who was just about to have some lunch helped by the older children. 'You look like 'Dora the Explorer'!' he announced.

My cheeks flushed, but I couldn't suppress the grin. 'Thank you,' I replied. 'Now, excuse me please.'

The office staff were on lunch and so I posted my timesheet through tiny gap in the glass, trusting them to sign and fax.

I breathed a sigh of relief as I slumped in my car.

Later on, at the supermarket, I'd just about collected all the bits I needed when I ran into someone I knew, apparently.

'Hi, you alright?' said this slim, blonde-haired woman.'

Was she talking to me? Indeed she was. I did the polite thing, 'Hi, y'alright?' All the time I was thinking to myself, when she gets home she's going to realise we don't actually know each other.

'Are you still on supply?'

Okay, maybe we did know each other. Or at least, she knew me. I chuckled, 'Yes, same old, same old.' She must have been from one of the hundreds of schools I'd been to. I wasn't really sure how I could narrow it down. I've been doing supply that long now that I've started to see teachers move from school to school and that confuses me even more.

'Sandra's just got a new job you know.'

'Really?!' Who on earth was Sandra? 'That's brilliant.' I was convinced by now that she recognised my face from doing the rounds of so many schools but she had got me mixed up with someone else.

'Anyway, I'll let you get on with your shopping. See you later, Carly.'

Yep. She definitely knew me then. To this day, I've no idea who she was, and it happens more often than you'd realise. Let's call it a hazard of the job.

I made my way to the checkouts, safe in the knowledge that the rest of the day would be spent thinking about none-school related things. I was happy to say that I'd survived, so that tomorrow I could yet again, supply another day.

ABOUT THE AUTHOR

Claire trained as a Secondary School Teacher and qualified in 2006. Her teaching experience thus far has been vast and varied with full time posts in both Primary and Secondary Schools, Private Tutoring at home and Supply Teaching all thrown in together. She has no intention of ever returning to full time teaching as she currently runs her own business in the Education Sector and really enjoys being a Supply Teacher.

Printed in Great Britain
by Amazon.co.uk, Ltd.,
Marston Gate.